Home

Home

Shana Chartier

Creators Publishing
Hermosa Beach, CA

CREATORS PUBLISHING
737 3rd St
Hermosa Beach, CA 90254
310-337-7003

Library of Congress Control Number: 2018937463
ISBN (print): 978-1-945630-81-1
ISBN (ebook): 978-1-945630-80-4

First Edition
Printed in the United States of America
1   3   5   7   9   10   8   6   4   2

For Patricia

Contents

Chapter One

Tara stared at the envelope, her numbness creeping its way toward upset.

It had been a long time since she had seen that address in the upper left hand corner, with its perfect script. She always did have the best handwriting. That's what an old-fashioned education brought you. Like cursive was even necessary anymore. Hadn't they stopped teaching it in Indiana? She couldn't be sure.

Finding the will to pull the paper from its sheath, she felt the familiar tinge of anger deep in her belly, coiling its way up to her heart like a venomous snake. After the fight with her mother three years ago, she had received angry-worded letters proclaiming her to be the worst daughter in the world. How dare she abandon her family? How dare she leave to go live her own life?

Of course, that last bit was Tara's words, not her mother's. It had been ages since her mother had deigned to send her hate mail, as she called it, and Tara found that to be a fantastic relief. Yet here she was, peering with trepidation at the next installment. She never responded to these diatribes. Why was her mother writing again now? She plopped down at her kitchen table. She unfolded the document and began to read.

Dear Tara,

I don't know if you plan on reading this. Not that you would. I don't recall ever getting a response from you. I suppose I shouldn't be surprised, given my past behavior, but I'm not going to take the blame for your terrible decisions.

That's not why I'm writing. I know we've had our differences, but you should know that in the time since you've left, I've been diagnosed with stage four cancer. The idiot doctor says I have three months to live, maybe less.

You can continue to ignore me if you want, but I wouldn't if I were you. Come home, Tara. If you don't, I will personally haunt you until the day you join me in the afterlife. I'm not kidding. Grow up, and let me see you one last time.

Your Beloved Mother,
Claire

Tara sat in bewilderment for a moment, which was very quickly followed by indignation. This was exactly like her mother. The conniving woman would do something like this — use her own death sentence as a blackmail tool to continue to try and control Tara's life. Unexpected tears sprang to her eyes.

Her mother was dying.

Tara had loved her mother, sometimes overwhelmingly so, but when the time had come to leave her life behind, she was anything but supportive. Tara fought back against memories of the shouting and the tears. She had spent so much time carefully pressing them out of her mind, wringing the memories from her head like water from a cloth.

In her twenty-five years of life, she had learned pretty quickly that happiness was not meant to last. Of course, she had been told that. She had seen it in the movies and read it in the thousand books she'd picked up since deciding to get a master's degree in library science.

And here was her choice, laid bare before her on cheap, white paper: Give up the only good while digesting the bad all over again, or lose it all by doing nothing. Tara wiped her moistened eyes, fearful and uncertain as she had been until the day she left home all those years ago. The memories began to rush in, and a piercing pain shot through the center of her forehead.

Tara sat alongside her sister, Ali, fear choking them both. The two little girls, one age seven and the other age nine, huddled together under a bush, waiting. Their cousin, a boy six years Tara's senior, had spent the past few hours convincing them that their grandmother's house was haunted. He went so far as to set up a series of tests that he sneakily controlled so they would live in fear that the spirits would be out to get them if they didn't follow him with his friends into the neighborhood. With a choice between the unseen phantoms and the visible outdoors of midnight, the girls chose that which they could comprehend. They followed him beyond the sparsely vegetated yard.

Sam Jr. had always tortured the girls in his own way. He pitched them against each other, causing fights that even in adulthood they never seemed to completely forgive or forget. It was as though he thrived off of the pain he could cause. And when he wasn't tormenting his young cousins, he was pinning a grasshopper to the wall, slowly twisting a needle into the poor insect as it writhed in unspoken agony.

And so it was that Tara and Ali clung together as their cousin threw eggs and toilet paper at the neighbors' homes, harming even more people. Finally, when he had had his fill, he guided the girls back to the house, where they gratefully embraced the sensation of safety once again.

Tara looked over to see Ali crying.

"What is it?" she whispered in a tremulous, tiny voice. Ali sniffed and glanced down but stayed silent. Tara followed her sister's gaze to find that she had wet herself from fear.

"Will you come to the bathroom with me?" Ali asked, ashamed. She needed to change her clothes but was scared of the dark-wooded bathroom where, hours before, they had seen golden leaves on a decorative tree blow without any wind. Another classic Sam Jr. prank. Tara nodded and stood guard at the bathroom door while Ali washed herself and changed into another pair of pajama pants. They then made their way to the homemade bed of old, ripped-up comforters, where Sam Jr. had already disrobed completely and fallen asleep.

Unwilling to get too close to him, Ali and Tara clung to a corner of the blanket, as far from him as possible. They tried to ignore the pungent fumes of cat urine that emanated from their unwashed, tattered bedding.

They waited until sleep finally came, hoping against hope that their parents would decide to come home from vacation earlier than planned.

That night, hot tears burned into a cool pillow as Tara cried herself to sleep.

•••

Chapter Two

As she jogged on the treadmill at the gym, Tara took a deep breath before deciding to confide in her closest friend, Cris.

"So I got a letter from my mother yesterday," she said, attempting at nonchalance and failing gratuitously. Cris saw right through her and began to fervently press at the buttons of her own treadmill. She slowed to a leisurely walk and stared at Tara, waiting for more.

"And?" she prompted. Tara didn't seem to get the hint with her dramatically slowing her workout for this juicy tidbit of information.

"She's dying," Tara said, her gaze forward. The sound of her lone treadmill pounded in her ears, so she finally tapped the buttons to meet Cris's pace. Cris rolled her eyes. She had heard all about Tara's mother's manipulation tactics over many, many glasses of cheap merlot.

"She's been dying since you first made plans to leave Colorado, Tara. Tell me something I don't know."

As she slowed her machine to a full stop, Tara reached for her gym bag, which she had tossed alongside the treadmill. Knowing that Cris would need proof, she procured the letter and handed it over for her to read. Cris turned off her own machine to focus and swiped the letter up with enthusiasm. She was the only one on the East Coast who really knew the whole story — and could understand. Cris had

battled her own demons with Tara's help. It was something they first
bonded over when their friendship began. Tara watched with
trepidation as she read every word, her expression shifting from doubt
to astonishment in less than a minute.

So my mother still has the gift, Tara thought. Cris gazed up
directly into her friend's eyes, concerned.

"So what are you going to do?" she asked. They must have
looked ridiculous standing in the middle of the gym doing nothing.
Cris wiped carelessly at a bead of sweat that had escaped from her
straight blond ponytail. Tara hesitated and tried to find her answer,
whatever it was.

"I don't know," she said with a sigh. "As much as my mom drove
me nuts, she's still my mom, Cris. I have so much unanswered anger,
and I just . . . I don't want to part ways with her knowing that what
happened between us was never resolved." Her eyes filled with tears
again. She had a feeling they'd be doing that a lot in the coming
months.

"I have to go back home," she said.

"You can't be serious!" Cris exclaimed as she gripped the bars of
her machine, her blond eyebrows darting straight up to her even
hairline. "You'd give up your dream job running the archive to go live
in Colorado? What will you do there?"

"I don't know," Tara mumbled, deflated. Of course, these were
all thoughts she had run over and over in her mind last night, to no
avail. There was no solution in this situation — not for her. No matter
what choice she made, her mother was still on death's doorstep. She
would have demons waiting for her, whether she faced them or not.
She could stay away and ignore the letter, like so many of the others
before, but deep down she knew she'd regret it for the rest of her life.

Cris continued to process Tara's dilemma at her own pace,
ignoring the defeated look on Tara's face.

"You don't know? Are you serious? Do you really think going
back to Denver is going to make everything better? And she could be

lying! This could be another desperate attempt to control you!" Cris looked disgusted, which made Tara feel just a tiny bit better, though she was loath to admit it to herself. Cris was good at truly appreciating the injustice of a situation when it happened to her friend. It was something Tara had always cherished about her.

"And let us not forget," Cris continued, "that time that she tried to call your college admissions office to get them to change their mind. Remember that? She tried to sabotage you from leaving in the first place, and you never would have found out if you weren't working in the records office. How many other secret ways has she tried to manipulate you? She made you go to every family event knowing how uncomfortable and upset it made you. She didn't care. You can't let her do this to you again."

"That's the thing, Cris. I don't think she would have done this if it weren't vital. She isn't that cruel."

Tara wondered even as she said it whether there was any truth to her words. Cris raised a critical eyebrow, entirely unconvinced.

"So . . . you'll just break your lease, give up your job, and go live at home like a teenager, then? How can you afford it?"

"I'm a librarian. It's not like my job is strictly local."

"I guess . . ."

She stared at Tara for what seemed an uncomfortably long time. Finally, she stepped forward on her machine and set it to a walking pace once again.

"I imagine you'll need help boxing up your apartment," she said, eyes straight ahead. Tara followed suit and restarted her machine, gazing forward at nothing in particular.

"I imagine I will."

"I like pepperoni on my pizza, and I want beer. But none of that cheap beer. You live on the third floor, woman, and I am not that cheap."

Tara smiled. This was why the East Coast was her home — Cris understood what it meant to be a family member. Unlike some people she knew . . .

"Noted," she said, a small smile barely touching the corner of her mouth. She wiped a stray long, brown curl away from her face and took a large gulp from her water bottle. Ever since the letter arrived, memories had been flooding in unwarranted. She tossed in her earbuds and slammed up the treadmill speed, trying to ignore the past. But her old repression tactics refused to keep working. Her feet pounded over and over, and her strong legs moved her ever forward, even as her mind slid back in time.

Tara sat in the corner of her Aunt Jo's lavish home, staring out at the adults with wary eyes. She had been brought to this this family gathering in spite of the party being more of an adult engagement, though she wished her parents had the good sense to just take her home. It was getting late, and the adults were getting drunker by the minute.

Dressed in baggy shorts and a softball T-shirt, Tara stood out like a sore thumb. Her aunts, who both had bleached hair and a coat of bronzer, considered her a blemish in every sense of the word. Whenever she tried to speak about her favorite sports or what she enjoyed learning at school, they would share a sarcastic, judgmental glance before backhandedly putting her down. They seemed to think her a complete idiot — some stupid twelve-year-old tomboy who understood nothing of the subtle nuances of catty judgment.

But Tara was nearly a teenager now, and her understanding of this form of communication had only increased as the girls at school outgrew their childlike love of friendship and took on meaner attitudes, including the distinct need to debase others as a way to prove superiority. Just last week, someone nonchalantly asked Tara whether she was a lesbian simply because of the way she dressed. She didn't know how to respond. No one in elementary school had bothered to notice how she dressed, and she was only first experiencing the joy of middle school politics and social cliques. That she liked boys seemed to be irrelevant; the girl had asked with such a smirk that it was obviously meant to be a put-down.

Two of the adults she was supposed to love unconditionally now treated her exactly the same way as the girls at school did. And it got worse when they drank. Tara was required to attend every family party — because family events were mandatory regardless of age or drinking ability. This event was particularly booze-filled, as it was a Valentine's Day party and the cocktails had a special theme. The upside to these kinds of parties was that she was generally able to hide and go unnoticed, the alcohol being a key distracter.

Tara huddled in the corner and tried to concoct a way to feign illness and have her mother drive her home, or at the very least order her a cab or something. As she glanced around, her mother was nowhere to be found. She sighed and rose to get a soda — anything to pass the time. As she made her way into the kitchen, she pulled a red Solo Cup from the top of the tower, holding the rest of the cups down to slide hers off. She spooned some ice into her cup and poured some Coke from an open bottle, tilting the cup in such a way to avoid too much fizz at the top. Glancing up, she noticed that a bouquet of fake flowers had caught fire and the flames were threatening to engulf the rest of the table.

She panicked, grabbed the base of the bouquet, and began to blow on it furiously. Though she had been placed in Girl Scouts, she had only been taught to sew and bake cookies, so she did not know that throwing dirt on the burgeoning flame would have been the best method to put it out. She blew and blew until the fire began to dissolve, fed by nothing but its remaining ashes. Suddenly, her wrist was caught in a viselike grip, and she whirled around.

"Don't blow out the candles, idiot!"

It was her aunt Marilyn, eyes glassy and shooting daggers with an accusatory glare. Her grip was only a little bit painful, and Tara said nothing. Rather, she held up the ruined bouquet for her aunt to see. It took a few minutes for her clouded mind to register that Tara was not actually blowing out the candles but rather preventing the house from going up in flames. She dropped Tara's hand, turning away and cackling to herself.

"Oh, my God. We almost set the house on fire!" she laughed to her sister, Jo, who in turn began cackling in a shrill chorus. Neither had noticed what Tara had done; neither cared.

Tara turned back to the table and blew out the candles for real. She wondered vaguely how two women who were painted so prettily could cackle like witches. It was then she began to understand what beauty actually meant.

Sweat poured from Tara's face, dripping in splotches on the ground. As she reached her milestone, she shut off her treadmill and music and waved goodbye to Cris, feeling completely and utterly spent. She entered the locker room, kicking off her shoes as she walked. She turned the shower nozzle to hot, stripped out of her sweaty clothing, and stepped beneath the firm, soothing pressure of the water. As she ran her hands along her slick hair, she resigned herself to her fate. There was nothing else for her to do now.

It was time to make the call.

•••

Chapter Three

"Mother?" she asked, her voice laced with caution.

She was reaching out into a cavernous void that had no foreseeable end in sight. She was met with what she assumed was stunned silence — which would be a first. She *had* heard her mother's voice saying hello just before, right?

"Hello?" she said.

"Yes, I'm here!" Claire said breathlessly.

More awkward silence. Tara racked her brain for something to say.

"So . . . I got your letter."

"Oh, good! So when can we expect you?" She was jumping right in, in control once again.

"Well, I can't just jump ship immediately, Mother," Tara spat out, unable to keep the venom out of her voice.

"Oh, don't be such a baby about it, Tara. Honestly, you're so oversensitive."

"So oversensitive that I'm being blackmailed to move back to a place I hate? No kidding. I really need to loosen up." The familiar burn of anger rose to her cheeks. The pretentiousness of her family was too much to bear. How would she do it again? She had finally gotten used to being free of her past.

"Well, we had to do something. So, I'll ask again: When should your father pick you up?"

That's right. Just breeze over it per usual, Tara thought grimly.

"I've given my boss notice to attempt a leave of absence. She can't promise that I'll have a job when this is over, but she said she'd try. That said, I've got a flight lined up for next week."

Colorado in the spring was way hotter than Boston. After Tara's conversation with her employer, she had dug out her warm-weather clothes while actively putting off this conversation. With such short notice, the flight wasn't exactly cheap either.

"That's wonderful news, Tara! Your father will be thrilled to see you. And the family, of course!"

Claire spoke with a false positivity, as though she were forcing herself to believe that somehow Tara would be willing and able to play happy family with the tyrants of her youth.

"Of course," Tara replied dryly. How Claire still managed to put on this charade was beyond her. She knew how her aunts really felt. How her grandmother felt. The only person she had ever been able to count on was her Gran, and she'd been gone a long time.

"Well, I'll let him know, and you just email us your itinerary so he doesn't have to wait for you. Glad you're on board with this, Tara. It's long overdue." The words were dripping with accusation.

The sheer nerve of the woman almost had Tara yelling for where she could put her offer before slamming the phone down. She used whatever semblance of sanity she had left to calm herself down and finish the conversation.

"Yeah, I will. Tell Dad I'll see him in a week."

"Will do, sweet pea! So long . . ."

Tara put down the phone as her mother crooned her last farewell. She sat back and sulked into her plush sofa. Gazing around, she took in every aspect of her apartment, trying to soak in the essence of the person she had become, the woman who would have to battle with the child she once was: desperate to escape and trapped in a false personality that denied her access to any form of happiness.

It was this thought that immediately alerted her to what was missing. She padded barefoot over to the kitchen, where a plugged bottle of red wine sat waiting to be poured. Pulling the stopper from the bottle, she poured the crimson liquid until it nearly reached the brim of the glass before raising her cup and placing it back on the counter. There would be no need to put the cork back in tonight, she mused. Her mother had that effect.

She plopped back down on the couch, determined to shut her brain off and completely avoid the coming trials. She saw her visage in the reflection of her small flat-screen TV: long brown hair, her father's blue eyes. She was, as her aunts had pointed out on many, many occasions, perfectly ordinary. She was average height for a woman, and she had an average build and a common shoe size. The only thing that was extraordinary about her, to her thinking, was her intelligence — on which her aunts, in all their gold-digging beauty, placed no value.

She favored sweatpants over all other clothing options and usually paired them with a sports bra and tank top. She ate relatively healthy but never denied herself treats — ice cream in particular. And, of course, red wine for nights just like this. Her apartment was a reflection of who she wanted to be: neat and clean, but homey. After meeting Cris, Tara spent many holidays and weekends at her parents' house in southern New Hampshire, where she developed a love for country furnishings and colonial culture. She spent her hard-earned savings on bargain couches, tables, and paintings, and rather enjoyed her farmhouse-style apartment right in the heart of the city. It was as far away from where she grew up as possible, just how she liked it.

Home, she thought, taking a gulp of wine. She was always excessively careful when people asked her where she was from: She was from Boston. She grew up in Colorado. Though many looked at her with confusion, to her mind, it made perfect sense. Boston was her home; Colorado was not. She was not from there in any way that made sense to her. It was something she came to terms with long ago.

Tara often pondered what it meant to be home. If home was where the heart resided, then she was doomed to exist as a wandering gypsy for life. Many of her closest friends — her *real* family, as she liked to think of them — had found jobs all across the United States, and a good part of her bank account was allocated for savings so she could see them as often as she could. At any given moment, she was missing someone, and though that should have been considered a gift — after all, one should feel grateful to have had such love in one's life — she couldn't help but feel the heaviness of her loss. She met people who bemoaned having all their family and friends in one place, always being in each other's business. And deep down, she wanted to give them a slap across the face. A loving family that cared about more than what was in your bank account or the makeup on your face? Didn't they realize what they had?

Of course, Tara wasn't against her entire pool of relatives. Other than her Gran, her sister had been a beacon of support through everything. They often spoke on Skype, where Tara was treated to chaotic sessions of attempting to talk to her nieces. The little girls were growing before her eyes but through the screen. She thought painfully of her own experiences growing up where they were and hoped that neither would suffer the same fate. She often reminded Ali not to expose her daughters to their aunts. Tara made a vow when they were born to make sure they felt the love she herself had always been denied. Still, deep down, Tara wondered whether her aunts would be kinder to her nieces, given their love for their mother.

Ali was the golden child of the family — the firstborn who loved being a girl and could spend days at a time at the mall, trying on clothes in every possible way until the right outfit came together. Their aunts adored her, and she had had many friends at school. She'd followed the politically correct path of feminine hobbies and activities growing up, followed by marriage, followed by beautiful, well-behaved children, and all by the age of thirty. Tara never resented her for that, though. All she wanted was a friend — someone to support her when hard decisions had to be made and loss was inevitable. Ali had always been that friend.

At least I'll get to be with them again, she thought in a grasp for optimism. Getting that time with her young nieces, the older two years old and the younger just a few months old, made the prospect a little less bleak.

When she looked down, Tara realized with slight surprise that she had finished her glass of wine. The warm buzz of relaxation washed through her limbs. She could do this, she realized in her slightly intoxicated haze. She was strong now! She had become more than they ever thought she could be.

She stood up and ran her hand along every piece of furniture on her way back to the kitchen, realizing that tomorrow she would have to start packing it up for storage. Luckily, her lease was up in a few weeks, so she had simply opted not to renew. *There's no going back,* she thought before grinning sarcastically at the double entendre. She had always assumed there would come a day when she would have to face her demons from whence they began. . . . She had just been putting that day off for as long as possible.

But it had found her. She poured half a glass more before putting the cork in the half-empty — no, half-full, to be optimistic — bottle. She continued to brush each crevice of furniture lightly with her fingertips on the way to her bedroom. Once there, she crawled underneath her patchwork quilt. She tried to fight the visions in her head. That damned letter opened up a spring well of stupid, unwanted memories.

Tara sat at Grandma Eve's scuffed-up wooden kitchen table, dressed in black. The week before, her uncle's wife had been driving in a rainstorm. She reached to the back seat for a can of soda, lost control of the car, and died. Another funeral. Death stood in every corner of every doorway Tara could remember knowing. This was how her family worked.

Eve's husband was Grandpa Jon, Tara's father's father, otherwise known to Tara as a member of the side of the family that disliked her for reasons she did not yet comprehend. Tara's earliest memories revolved around the hospital waiting room, as Grandpa Jon suffered from heart failure and was often admitted. This did not deter him from being an opinionated, unsocial businessman. He had started his own software company and launched it off the ground, becoming a successful entrepreneur. And he'd hired her father to be his replacement after his death. Of course, Grandpa Jon was always dying.

Tara had become so familiar with hospitals that she had even begun to win the card games on the Styrofoam hot chocolate cups — a feat that didn't seem to be a common occurrence. The final year was truly the worst. His tenth heart attack left his heart in tatters. If he wanted to live, a transplant was the only solution.

Her family debated the pros and cons of this decision. He was in his early sixties, so the likelihood of even getting a donor was slim. There was also the chance something could go wrong during the operation and he'd be a vegetable — a possibility he vehemently detested. They bickered and argued over the dying man, and he listened in a daze, with one foot on the other side of death.

As they stood by his hospital bedside, Aunt Jo stepped forward and announced that she was pregnant. Not only that, she wanted her unborn child to know his grandfather and love him for the dashing and wonderful person he was. Having never received any particular attention or praise from the man, Tara tried to take her word for it. Between Jo's desire to have a grandfather for her baby and Grandma

Eve's desire not to be a widow, the decision had been made. Surprisingly, a heart was found for him, and the surgery took place.

The year following that decision had been one of the worst of Tara's life. Every day passed with some time spent at the hospital, the cold fragrance of sanitation seeping into her skin. Sometimes he remembered who they were, and sometimes he didn't. One day, when they walked in, they saw that his legs had turned charcoal black from the knee down. The blood wasn't circulating properly in his heart, and his legs were amputated that very night.

Still, Grandpa Jon was a stubborn, headstrong man. He fought every day to recover, to get back home and continue working. He got a cheap pair of prosthetic legs, though he mostly wore them as he was pushed around in a wheelchair. He insisted that everything stay exactly as it was and demanded that no special treatment be given to him — with one exception. Since he was dying, and had been since before Tara was born, apparently, the family was expected to be together most of the time. This included all holidays, all weekends, and most evenings after school or work. At every meal, Jon ate whatever was put in front of him before slowly gagging it back out into a paper towel. They still went out to eat, and Tara watched balefully as the people seated at the tables around them lost their appetite and left, leaving her and her family to pretend openly that they couldn't hear the chokes at the head of the table.

And so it was that Tara came to be sitting next to her sister in their grandparents' kitchen, staring out the glass door that led to the balcony. The Rocky Mountains coated the horizon with a light bluish-gray and were surrounded by the brown, polluted world of suburbia. At night, you could see a lit-up cross on one of them, which branded them as some sort of religious monument. Tara preferred it around Christmastime, when the cross was replaced with a giant glowing star. Her thoughts were dissolved by the slight sound of gagging to her left. Grandpa Jon spit up whatever he had been eating and then gazed up at Ali, his eyes bright, even grandfatherly.

"My God, Ali. You're getting more and more beautiful every day. I can't believe you're my granddaughter," he said. His voice sounded like tinfoil on a chalkboard. He then glanced over at Tara with darkened icy-blue eyes and furrowed brows, and said nothing.

It wasn't an unfamiliar gaze, but to have a dying husk of a man still treat her with extra debasement hurt more than Tara was willing to admit. She got up from the table and walked away.

Tara threw a pillow across the room. She grabbed another, pulled it over her head, and tried to think of something else — anything else. Tomorrow, she would pack. Tonight, she would simply be.

● ● ●

Chapter Four

Her flight stopped over at Chicago's O'Hare Airport, where a delay was inevitable. She walked to the glowing wall of screens, saw the red lettering next to her flight number, and knew it was going to be one of those days. She updated her dad with the new arrival time and headed straight for the bar in search of a Sam Adams Cherry Wheat. As she took a seat, a young bartender approached, took her order, and placed a frosty bottle on a white napkin before heading off to help other customers. Cherry Wheat was one of her favorites — the right combination of crisp and sweet — and she drank it with relish, savoring each sip as if it, too, would prolong her departure.

She watched travelers come and go — parents with children, couples, soldiers, salt-and-pepper-haired white men in suits who would most likely be populating the priority-seating red carpet. *Plus ca change, plus c'est la meme chose*, she thought. *The more things change, the more they stay the same.* She wondered whether her return to Littleton would be like that. How much of her former world would be different? As she took another sip of her beer, she felt a brush against her back.

"Excuse me," said a male voice behind her. She glanced back absently, mumbled that it was fine, and turned back to her beer. On the television hanging above the bar, one politician was angrily blaming another for the world's problems. She steered her gaze away. There was enough drama in her life at present — no need to add national crises to it.

"You live around here?"

Tara turned to discover that the man had sat beside her at the crowded bar. He was young, probably in his late twenties, with a slightly crooked nose and full black hair. His eyes were shockingly blue, almost the color of Arctic ice. He had a rugged look about him, and seemed likable and down-to-earth. Tara recovered.

"Um, no. Actually, I'm from Boston," she said.

"Really? You don't have an accent," he observed. He glanced around the bar until he caught the blond female bartender's attention and ordered a Coors Light. She smiled at him and slid a frothy pint to him across the counter.

Tara hesitated. She was never sure how much information to give at this point. Her accent had come into question several times, and depending on who it was, she would be willing to provide different information. Being that this was a stranger at an airport, she decided it was unlikely she had anything to lose by telling him a little bit. His blatant attractiveness didn't really hurt either, said the beer in her system.

"I spent my formative years in Colorado, so that's probably why." His expression lit up like the Fourth of July.

"Get out! I'm from Boulder! I'm on my way back now, from a trip to Vermont," he beamed. If there was one thing Coloradans loved, it was being from Colorado. But she did not fit into that category. Being used to the game, she smiled politely. Of course she had to sit next to a Coloradan — today of all days. Luckily, he was traveling from a place she happened to love, so she clung to that and went with it.

"Vermont is beautiful this time of year," she said, figuring the weather would be the best conversation topic for a passing stranger.

"It is. Plus, they have some of the best farming culture I've ever seen. I've learned a lot!"

"You're a farmer?"

"I am. Early to bed, early to rise!"

"You seem irrationally cheerful for someone who just confessed to being an early riser," she said with a smirk. His positive nature was contagious, and she was actually starting to like this person. After all, he wasn't related to her, so that put him one step ahead of the game. He grinned back.

"Well, what is it they say? I'll sleep when I'm dead? I don't particularly see it that way. I do like naps, but life is about making the most of it, I think."

"I can see that," she said, returning back to her beer.

"So . . . who died?" he asked without preamble. She looked back up at him, surprise etched on her face.

"What?"

He took a sip of beer and stared at her over the rim of the glass, his eyes holding a teasing glint. He finished his drink and carefully placed the glass back on the bar.

"I said, 'Who died?' You've been sulking into your beer for a good ten minutes now, so I figured there must be a funeral or something tragic that you have to go to. . . . I hope it was no one close to you."

She paused, considering her answer.

"You've been watching me for ten minutes?" She didn't want to confide in this happy-go-lucky farmer. He obviously had no idea what it was like to be forced to face your demons. He was probably the type of man who let phone companies take advantage of him because he didn't want to be mean. He didn't need to know why she was openly sulking any more than some other stranger. However, none of this seemed to register, because his smile stayed in place and seemed genuine.

"Well, maybe not you in particular. I've been looking for a spot at the bar for the last ten minutes, so naturally, I got a good look at everyone sitting down. Lucky for you, this was the seat that opened up!"

"Yeah, I certainly do have that kind of luck," she mumbled.

"You're skirting my question, which I think means no one has died. So what gives? You might as well confide in me, a compassionate and temporary friend at the bar. What have you got to lose?"

She pondered for a moment. *Well, he does have a point.*

"I'm going home," she blurted, almost choking on the forbidden word. He looked confused.

"Isn't that a good thing? Home is where you feel safe and loved, and everyone plays games and helps each other out. I don't see the problem."

She laughed dryly.

"I see your definition of home and mine are distinctly different, good stranger," she said, taking a gulp of beer, mostly for dramatic effect. She was the woebegone, mysterious stranger minding her own business — country western style. Where was a gunshot or a distracting bar fight when you needed one?

"Tom."

"Tom?"

"Yeah, that's my name. Tom Sanders, the annoying farmer who won't leave you alone until you smile for real."

"That's a long name. You should really consider cutting it down a bit, Tom Sanders, the annoying farmer who won't leave me alone until I smile for real," she shot back. She realized that she was starting to have fun with Tom Sanders. He just laughed.

"Well, I'll consider it. Although, it would be helpful also knowing your name — unless you would like me to call you Sulky Bar Girl, which actually has a nice ring to it."

"Sulky Bar Girl. . . . Hmm, I like that. It fits me very appropriately at the moment, and since our twenties are the time to have an existential crisis, it seems apt. Well done, Tom Sanders." She smiled and went for another sip only to realize her bottle was empty. She met the female bartender's eyes and had a fresh, cold beer placed before her. Suddenly, Tom's face lost some of its joviality, and he turned his body to face her more directly.

"Really, though. You look down, and sometimes people are brought into other people's lives at just the right moment to help them out. I think this might be one of those moments," he said.

Tara stared into the narrow spout of her beer as she considered his words. Her frown deepened ever so slightly before she opted to keep her information to herself awhile longer. Besides, flirting was more fun, anyway. Her lip curled up as she met his gaze again.

"Your words are so wise and true. So what can I help you with in your life, Tom Sanders?" Tom's blue eyes narrowed as he took another sip.

"Well, I met this girl very recently. I can tell she's upset about something, and I'd like to help her, but she's really private about it. Also, we're going to the same destination, so there is a very strong chance I could be sitting next to her on the flight and proceed to poke the side of her head for the next two-and-a-half hours until she decides to tell me what's wrong," he said, smiling triumphantly at the finish.

"You wouldn't!" she exclaimed, mock-scandalized.

"I would," he said, his gaze boring into her. It was so intense that she was tempted to look away, but she held it. She was not the girl she once was; she would stand up to anyone, as their equal. Finally she sighed, conceding victory, and held out her hand.

"Tara Kingston," she said, feeling the warmth of his hand as he slid it into hers and gave it a firm shake. His skin was dry and calloused, exactly what she would expect of a farmer.

"See? Now that wasn't so hard, was it?"

"A lot easier than getting a genuine smile."

"Darn. And that was a pretty big challenge." He looked at her pensively. "I think you'd better tell me what's wrong first so I know what I'm battling against. Maybe define home for me from your personal handheld dictionary."

My, he's persistent, she thought. But his frivolity had worked; her defenses had come down . . . slightly.

"Define home?" she said, starting to feel the burn, which always intensified when alcohol was involved. "Home is where my mother is asking me to return and forcing me to deal with my relatives, who, for all intents and purposes, are the reason I have few fond memories of my childhood. Home is a place where people are self-absorbed and rude, and I have to pretend to be okay with it, because otherwise my father gets upset."

Tara looked away, lost in her own misery.

She continued, "Since he has been financially responsible for me, coming to my rescue all of my life, I feel a debt to him that I believe will never be paid. My grandmother on my mother's side was the kindest to me, and without her I wouldn't be who I am today."

It was as though a tap had been turned on, and the words continued to pour out of her. She took a steadying breath.

"She died. Now my mom is dying. It's a three-month death sentence, in fact. You see, in my home, family members use death as a way to control their children and grandchildren, and it is oh so effective." She gripped her beer so tight it seemed the glass would shatter.

She didn't want to look Tom in the face, to see the judgment she knew would be there after this show of bitterness and baggage. Her curiosity won out, though, and she peeked over at him. She saw sympathy, curiosity, and concern all somehow mingling on his features. This made her feel much worse. She had learned long ago not to wait for anyone's sympathy. Everyone had their own sob story — well, maybe not Sun Beam Tom — and she was not the exception.

She was the rule. If she were having a pity party, she knew she'd get over it once she got back to her own life on the East Coast. Chances were she'd be back home by Christmas anyway.

"Wow," he said, taking in her rant. She imagined he would be on his way now. . . . Maybe she should have told him in the first place — saved him all that flirtation with a woman who clearly had too much baggage to be datable.

"Surprisingly, your definition of home really sucks," he said. So he did understand the finer points of melancholy; he had some realist in him. Interesting. She suddenly liked him a little bit more.

"Yeah, it really does," she conceded.

"But I have some great news for you," he said.

"Oh yeah? What's that, Tom Sanders?" Her bill had arrived, and the flight was getting ready to board. Time flies when you're being accosted by the happiness police. She gave the bartender her card and watched her walk about with the bill.

"You have another friend in Colorado now! Me."

She stared at him, this stranger who opened up to her at a bar in an airport. Actually, he hadn't opened up at all, yet somehow he had managed to harvest the most personal secrets out of her. Sneaky. Tara had been bruised enough by men to realize a weapon when she saw one. His happened to be a smile and some charm. But she'd been fooled by that before. She gave him a nod as she filled in a tip for the overpriced beers and dropped the pen back down.

"Trust me, Tom Sanders. You don't want to be a part of what I'm walking into," she said, hefting her carry-on bag over her shoulder. She began walking toward the gate. There was more to focus on than flirting — she had to mentally prepare to spend quality time with her mother. What could be more exciting?

"Trust me, Tara Kingston. Having a friend hold you to the ground in a tornado is much better than flying off alone. Didn't you see *Twister?*"

Somehow he had caught up to her already.

"You are very persistent," she said, trying to sound annoyed. But she didn't pull it off. He just smirked.

"It's like I said. I have arrived in your life at just the right moment — to help you slay the dragon!"

"Does that make you the prince?"

"Only if you're into that kind of thing," he said, wagging his dark eyebrows. Tara realized that the man had no shame. It was fantastic.

"I'll let you know." She shifted her bag on her shoulder as a woman's voice came on the speaker to announce the boarding. Tilting her head toward the gathering crowd, she beckoned him to follow her.

"Well, come on then, you lost puppy. I can't just leave you in this airport grinning all by yourself. I'm not that cruel." His face lit up again. He diligently fell in stride, and they waited for their group to be called. Tara wished in that moment that she had met him at any other time. She could have actively participated in his excessive optimism. As it was, the Tara who lived in Boston, who hosted parties and facilitated all sorts of games, happened to be dormant. That person always hid at the sight of a family gathering and was replaced by a cool-headed intellectual determined to prove her worth to the people who had crushed her confidence as a child.

"Where are you sitting?" Tom asked, holding out his ticket. He was in 8A, the seat right after first class. Tara had not been so lucky, having procured a ticket only a week prior. She held up her ticket for him to see. 23F. He looked disappointed.

"Well, maybe we can get someone to change seats once we get settled," he reasoned, mostly to himself.

Tara wondered what it was about her that could have possibly attracted a man like Tom Sanders. He was attractive. He seemed well-rounded, like one of those people who life hadn't disappointed so much that they faced the world with absolute caution and disbelief, waiting for their hopes to be dashed once again. It was rare for Tara to meet anyone like that, and here he was following the mopey archivist. It didn't make any sense to her, but she was in no position to question it now. It actually felt good to have someone from the outside cheering her through this. Maybe he was right; maybe she did need an anchor in the perfect storm she was about to sail into.

The woman with the microphone announced Tom's group, and he hesitated.

"You can go. I promise I'll be able to make it through the flight — my enemies aren't on the plane," she said, trying a weak attempt at a joke. His lip curled upward, which revealed a very handsome, boyish dimple, and then he walked up and beeped his ticket through. Tara waited for all the other groups to be called before making her way forward. As she passed him on the plane, she noticed the flight was completely full. He looked at her with regret as he glanced to either side of him, both seats filled. She gave him a small *it's okay* shrug and trekked her way back to 23F, which, as she had suspected, was very close to the toilets.

Well, she thought, *it wouldn't be a trip to Denver without Tara hidden in the back where she belongs.* She scooted past the portly gentleman taking up the aisle seat and leaned heavily against the double-paned window. Fortunately, she had always been the kind of person who could sleep on planes, and she rested her forehead against the wall as she cast one last baleful stare at the airport tarmac. She closed her eyes and allowed herself to drift off to sleep.

• • •

Chapter Five

Tara was dreaming.

•

She sat at her Gran's kitchen table, openly deflated. Gran was
pulling the final baking sheet from the oven, a steaming batch of
peanut butter cookies waiting to be cooled and eaten. They had been
a family favorite for as long as Tara could remember. The air was
radiant with the sweet scent. The kitchen table was adorned with a
bright-yellow cloth, and resting atop it in a refreshingly old-fashioned
way was her grandmother's white china teapot, complete with delicate
china teacups. Tara's grandfather had spent his younger years in the
military, and Gran had picked up this European habit while living
abroad when they were first married. Tara loved to hear her stories,
especially when she was having a hard time with her father's side of
the family. They were soothing and allowed her to dream about
escape.

Today's melancholy was not a result of her aunts' usual disregard
for her self-esteem. Since starting high school, she had tried to
become part of a group — any group — and somehow managed to fail
miserably. She had auditioned for the choir and tried out for the
softball team, soccer team, and dance team . . . pretty much any team
available. Today's pity-party theme was her rejection by the yearbook

club. She had been asked to do a writing sample about anything, and she was so proud of the piece she painstakingly put together. Her interview was uneventful, except that the woman asking questions made a very peculiar comment that Tara couldn't get out of her mind.

"What do you see as a potential challenge in joining this club?" she asked, pencil poised above her notebook. Tara thought for a minute and then decided to be absolutely honest.

"Frankly, getting in. I was one of the most successful hitters on my youth softball team, but I can't get in here. I was asked to sing the national anthem for a Colorado Rockies game, and yet I didn't make the choir. I don't know what it takes to be included here. I just don't. Writing is the one thing I know I'm good at, so here I am." The woman stared at her. Tara was wearing a nice black skirt and a purple button-down top for the occasion. She hoped looking professional would help her cause.

"You don't know anyone?" the woman finally asked.

"I'm sorry?" Tara said. The woman look annoyed.

"I said, 'You don't know anyone?' In order to get into a club or a team, you have to have the right connections. It doesn't hurt being a senior either."

"What about natural talent?" Was this woman seriously implying that the only way to get into extracurricular activities here — which, in this competitive day and age, was vital to getting into a decent college — was to network and play politics?

The woman scoffed. "Natural talent doesn't count if you don't understand the playing field, Tammy."

"It's Tara. You are a grown adult, and you see no issue with this?" Tara was incredulous.

"You might as well learn the ways of the world now, kid. It doesn't matter how good you think you are; you're nothing without connections."

"I see," she said, annoyed at the sharp sting developing behind her eyes. Tara had no connections. No one here seemed to be able to tolerate her except for her tired, overworked teachers, and even they could rarely put in the time to help her grow beyond academics.

"You're welcome to try again in a few years," the woman said. Tara picked up the social cue and stood, brushing her hands down her front to smooth out her skirt before stiffly walking out.

Faced with more grueling disappointment, she drove over to Gran's and cried bitterly as she sat at her warm and inviting kitchen table. Gran listened first, giving her hand a firm squeeze, and then offered supportive commentary before starting on the cookies. She always listened before offering advice or comfort, and her opinion mattered more to Tara than anyone else's for that reason. Gran paused to bring a plate of hot cookies to the table and fill the teapot with hot water.

"So you've been given an obstacle. Life is filled with them, Tara. What you need to learn now is how to make lemonade," she said as she poured their tea. Milk and two sugars were always added. It was a sweet afternoon treat. Tara took a small bite of a cookie and relished in its flavor before answering.

"I can't make lemonade from rotten lemons, Gran. The taste won't sit well."

"Don't get smart with me, Miss Tara," Gran said, giving Tara a playful slap on the wrist. Tara smirked begrudgingly. "Now tell me what your solution is."

"There isn't a solution. I've tried everything. I hate this place and everything about it. I just want to travel, like you did!"

"Traveling like I did was fine and well, Tara, but I didn't do it to run from my problems like a coward. You're sixteen now. It's time to start problem-solving. Decisions and happenings are only going to get more difficult from here, so if you can't handle it now, you won't make it. Period." She took a sip of tea, completely unperturbed by the harsh meaning behind her gentle words. Tara didn't mind her form of honesty, though, since it was in her best interest and not used to make her feel small. She considered this piece of wisdom while reaching for another cookie.

"I guess I could look for something outside of school," she said slowly, the thought having snuck into her mind. Gran's smile reached up to her eyes.

"Now you're getting it. Your father makes plenty of money, and your happiness matters. He can dish out a little extra for you to be in a club."

"I guess." All she really wanted was to bide her time until she could leave for college. She had learned long ago that school was her only ticket out, and if she were to do well enough, she could get a scholarship to somewhere far, far away. Of course, the thought of leaving Gran was unbearable. . . . Maybe she would come with. It was a nice thought, having Gran with her always.

"You guess nothin'! Take control of your life, Tara. You can't help the way others treat you, but you can certainly help the way you treat yourself. If you have regrets, if you let life's challenges defeat you and bring you down, how will you feel at the end knowing you had time to make your life what you wanted but bent to the will of others instead?"

"Yes, Gran," Tara said obediently. Gran was right. She was letting her situation define who she was, rather than fighting it. But how was she, a sixteen-year-old girl, supposed to fight anything? Her only feasible solution was to take flight and learn how to be who she wanted to be with a clean slate. There had to be some places where merit mattered over connections — at least she fervently hoped so.

After finishing her tea, Gran stood and made her way toward the living room.

"Come on, then. Let's get your mind off it in the usual way," she said, marching over to the large, comfy sofa that faced her brick fireplace. She reached around the side for the basket of knitting supplies and sat. Gran had taught the girls to knit when they were little, and she firmly believed that it was a form of meditation as well

as a useful ability. Practical life skills, she had said, were not to be
forgotten in this age of dependence on a glowing screen. Tara
followed and picked out her blue ball of yarn, at the end of which was
a project quickly becoming a new pair of slippers.

With all the wildfires, Colorado was dry as dead wood, and it
burned just the same. Traditional fireplaces had been outlawed some
time ago, so Gran's was merely for show. She made up for it by
buying some decorative candleholders and lighting tea lights on
occasion. This room had much the same feel as the kitchen,
showcasing the bright, happy colors of spring and summer. Tara felt
as though a breath of fresh air passed through her just by being there,
which was why she came as often as possible. Sometimes it seemed
like Gran would forever be her only friend, but that didn't sting as
much when she was here as it did when she was at school.

They settled in with their knitting projects and sat in comfortable
silence for a while, enjoying the peacefulness of busy hands in the act
of creation. Tara finally calmed down. So what if high school was a
pain in the ass? At least she had her smarts. She already knew she'd
be able to escape. . . . It was just hanging in there that was the hard
part. Gran had always said that life was a series of peaks and troughs,
and that the struggles were created to develop an appreciation for
when things finally got better. In essence, the bad was necessary to
understand what was good. Tara had tried to see it that way, but when
you were stuck in the middle of the bad, it was harder to see that there
might be rhyme or reason to it.

"Hey, Gran?"

"Yes?"

"Will you come to college with me, wherever I get in?" she
asked, half smiling. It was a ridiculous request, one she knew would
be shut down, but that didn't stop her from asking. Gran didn't look
up from her knitting and continued her stitches as she answered.

"What would I do that for? I already have enough binge-drinking
parties here."

Tara sighed. "I suppose you do." The only parties Gran had involved her cats and a glass of wine.

Gran paused for just a moment and patted Tara's knee. "Don't you worry, Tara-Bee. I'll be on call for whatever comes your way, and I'll embarrass you with the loudest whistle at your graduation, just like always."

Tara laughed. Her grandmother had always been the first — the only — person to make her feel special. She looked forward to the day she could blush as Gran cheered her across the stage.

If only she had known then that that day would never come.

•

Tara woke to popping in her ears as the plane descended into Denver International. She gazed blearily out the window, taking in the circle and square patches of land that quilted the earth. The mountains loomed in the distance — the direction of her final destination finally visible. She stretched as far as the cramped space would allow, tilting her stiff neck from side to side and wincing as it made muted cracking noises. Sleeping upright did have its downfalls, namely the 12-hour ache afterward.

She waited patiently for everyone else on the plane to grab their carry-ons and shuffle forward, and then finally took her turn gliding up the aisle. The airport was the same as she remembered; it had a distinct scent that she could never fully describe. Maybe it was simply altitude. She spotted Tom waiting for her by the walking escalator in the terminal, looking spry as ever. She noticed how casually he wore his white collared shirt, sleeves rolled up to the elbows, and his dark denim jeans. His waterproof hiking boots solidified his persona of countryman. He waved at her, and she nodded her head in acknowledgment as she made her way over.

"Great flight, huh?" he asked. She reminded herself to ask what kind of drugs he was on and where she could get some.

She rubbed some of the sleep from her eyes. "Yeah, just super," she said yawning. He looked at her with jealousy in his eyes.

"You're one of those people who can sleep on planes and in cars, huh?"

"Guilty," she said with a smirk. They proceeded toward the escalator that would take them down to the tram, where Tara would have to start looking for her father in baggage claim. She whipped out her phone and sent him a quick text to let him know she had arrived.

"Cool," he replied. Dad was never big with words.

"I'd love to be able to do that," Tom continued, "but I can never seem to get comfortable without being totally horizontal."

This statement made Tara think of what Tom would be like "horizontal," and she blushed at the thought. Where did that come from? She glanced at him, and he gave her a knowing smirk. The bastard did it on purpose. And she didn't have time for this kind of crap, not with a jail sentence over her head before a trip back to the East Coast. Now, if he were from Boston . . .

The tram stopped at the terminal, and Tara strode over to the towering uprising escalator, glancing balefully at the decorative paper airplanes strung above. She braced herself to see her father again for the first time in three years. What would he say? *Hi, Tara. Thanks for ignoring your mother's terminal illness all this time. Oh, and by the way, you're a terrible daughter, and we plan on making you pay for it while you're here.* One could only assume.

"It'll be all right, you know," Tom said from the step above her.

"I appreciate your assurance, but believe me, you have no idea what will be all right," she shot back. Who was he to say such a thing? Mr. Happy-Go-Lucky Farmer. She saw him shrug from the corner of her eye.

"Maybe. Maybe not. Just know that even when family sucks, sometimes they have a way of surprising you."

"Maybe yours does. Mine isn't big on change."

"Well, you just never know," he said, undeterred in his belief that she'd somehow come out of this for the better. She wished she could share some of his optimism.

"You really are persistent, aren't you?" she asked with a huff, her shoulders slumping. He just laughed.

"Well, I did say I wouldn't give up until I got a genuine smile from you, so positivity seems to be my only option here."

"I should say so."

The tall escalator was reaching its peak now, and Tara noticed Tom beginning to shift from one foot to another, uncharacteristically uneasy.

"Maybe we should exchange numbers — you know, for when you need my unfailing optimism to guide you through this trial- and tribulation-filled period of life."

They reached the top and were momentarily blinded by the bright-white interior of the airport. Tara moved over to one side, out of the river of people searching for their ride home. She gave Tom one long, searching look. Above him, the white canvas-like airport structure towered like a large, old-timey circus tent. He seemed genuinely scared that she wouldn't actually give him her number. Was he really capable of insecurity after all this show of bravado? It made him all the more endearing, though she doubted he'd actually be a part of her life after this moment. Men never called, or if they did, they called too much, and it became obsessive and creepy. Giving him her number meant taking a chance on one of those possibilities.

"You promise not to be a weird stalker just pretending to be a nice guy? You *are* a Coloradan, so I can't fully trust you." He crossed his heart in a boyish gesture of trust before lifting two fingers held together.

"Scout's honor. I will only call occasionally, when I sense I might be needed," he said. The humor in his eyes blended with his sincere honesty was a cocktail Tara realized she could get used to.

"All right, Tom Sanders. Give me your phone." He handed it over, and she typed her name and number and saved it. She then called herself and saved his information so she would know what 303 number was calling her . . . and that it wasn't a family member. The long line of people waiting for their loved ones began to dissolve, and Tara glanced up to see her father waiting patiently behind the metal barrier. She gave a small wave, and he nodded. She turned back to Tom.

"Well, it's been real," she said, sticking out her hand. He took it and held it firmly, his warm, calloused farmer's hand molding perfectly to hers.

"Good luck, Tara Kingston. I really hope it's not as bad as you think it will be." He squeezed her hand.

"You and me both." He held on for slightly longer than was necessary before letting her go, and she turned to head toward her father.

"Hey, squirt," he said. That was the pet name he had given her as a child. He gave her a side hug as they fell in step — the most affection he had been able to develop as he aged — and she side-hugged him back.

"Hey, Dad." She kept it simple, just as he liked it.

As they waited for her two large suitcases to appear on the belt, he asked, "Good flight?"

"I think so . . . slept through everything but the landing."

"You were always a good sleeper." He nodded as she pointed to one of her bags and then the other, and each of them hefted one onto the ground. He led the way to the parking lot, and they walked the rest of the way in silence. When they reached his car, Tara couldn't help but comment.

"Another Audi?" she said. He looked pleased. If there was one thing her father could talk about, it was cars. He had leased them and traded them out since before she could remember. Her least favorite was the Stealth. Being the youngest, she was always crammed behind the driver's seat. Her dad was six feet two inches tall with long legs. . . . Needless to say, she was excited when he traded that in for a car that allowed her to put her feet down.

"Yep," he answered. "Best car they got right now. It's a smooth ride." More silence ensued as they shoved one of her suitcases in the trunk and the other in the back seat before sliding in and heading over the I-70 to the house. He was right — it was a smooth ride. As they drove, she couldn't sit still or take more of his usual silence, so she tried to initiate conversation. It was better than sitting and waiting for the inevitable confrontation with her mother.

"So, how are things?"

"Same," he said. He was never willing to further the conversation longer than he had to. No one could ever accuse Bob Kingston of being a gossip.

"Really?" She couldn't believe that he had literally no news on the past three years. *Something* must have happened that was worth talking about. He glanced over at her.

"We renovated the bathroom. It's got a nice whirlpool tub now. Works good."

"Well, that *is* good news." Some things really didn't change, and though her father didn't seem to hold a grudge against her three-year disappearance act, it was as though he hadn't even noticed she was gone. She couldn't decide which was worse. She obviously had to have meant something to these people for her mom to use her own illness as collateral to get her to come home, right?

The mountains loomed ever closer as the two made their way to the suburbs.

"Your mom's not doing too well, Tara," he said after another few minutes of silence.

"What?" she asked, her mind rejoining her body from wherever it had wandered off to.

"Her cancer. It's why she's gone all mental in forcing you back here. She doesn't think she has a lot of time." His face remained calm, like this were ordinary news. There had never been any doubt that Tara belonged to this man; she was his female likeness in every

physical way. Hair, skin, eyes, nose . . . all of it was the same, minus
the small bald spot at the crown of his head.

"How much time does she have, really?" She knew she should
be more sympathetic, but after a lifetime of guilt trips and mind
games, the proverbial boy had cried wolf one too many times. Her
father, the realist, might actually give her an honest answer. He looked
over at her, and for the first time, she saw the weariness in the depths
of his eyes. It was eerie, as though she were staring into her own. He
rubbed a hand through his thinning brown hair, and she noticed a
peppering of gray near his temples that wasn't there before. Maybe
things were worse than she thought.

"I don't know," he finally answered. "You know how doctors are.
. . . One day they've got an answer, the next they don't. It's all about
keeping us coming so they can get our money."

"I don't think that's why, Dad. Cancer isn't exactly the easiest
thing to monitor." *And you should know that,* she thought bitterly. To
her surprise, that riled him up. A reddish hue blossomed on his
cheeks.

"Well, they damn well should know more by now!" he said,
pounding his fist against the steering wheel and then falling into angry
silence. Tara was stunned and said nothing. A sense of impending
doom fell over her, and her heart filled with dread. They rode the rest
of the way without saying a word.

Tara's parents had lived in the same house for about five years,
since their girls had gone off to school. Tara was grateful not to have
to return to her childhood home. Knowing she would have to spend
time at Grandma Eve's house was bad enough. At least her parents'
place wasn't filled with decades of nasty memories. The new house
was built recently and looked a lot like every other cookie-cutter
house in the region: a mixture of wood and brick, a gas fireplace just
for show, granite countertops and wood cabinets. Earth tones ruled,
and each two-car garage mirrored the next in a long line of adherence
to normalcy. One thing she had always appreciated about her parents'

move was that neither she nor her sister had had to give up their room for a home gym — there would always be an open bedroom if they were to ever need it.

They pulled into the paved driveway, and Tara's father carefully parked his baby inside the garage, where it would be safe and free of risk from elemental damage. Tara exhaled, not having realized that she was holding her breath. *Well, here we go*, she thought, and a sense of finality settled over her. She took the suitcase from the back seat and lugged it in behind her father, who had taken the other from the trunk. Although he was in his midfifties, the man was still strong as an ox and never complained about anything. Tara still admired that about him and tried to emulate it in her adult life.

As she stepped into the house, she braced herself for some kind of fight or confrontation. The last time she spoke to her mother here didn't go well. Tempers were high, and Tara promised at the top of her voice never to come back again.

She let go of her suitcase handle and cautiously walked into the kitchen, where she saw her mother sitting at the round nook table.

Claire had once been a strong, even muscular woman, but a frail and flaccid figure had taken her place. The skin on her arms drooped a little; it was transparent in the sunlight coming through the windows. She was paying her bills, and she glanced up when she heard Tara enter. She hesitated, contemplating her next move, and then slowly rose and looked her daughter directly in the eye. She seemed standoffish. Tara assumed she could see the complete and utter shock on her face. She couldn't hide it. What had happened to her mother in the short time she had been away?

"Take a good look, Tara. It's not like how it happened to her, but it's taking me all the same."

Tara found her voice, somehow forgetting the anger that usually rose when her mother spoke to her with such condescension.

"Why didn't you tell me?" she nearly whispered. Her upset seemed to move something inside her mother, and her expression softened.

"I didn't want to face it, Tara. Your father kept telling me to get tested, but I didn't want to hear what they would say. Maybe if I had, I wouldn't be so far along."

She walked slowly toward Tara, stopping a short distance away from her. There was a gap between them that was three years wide. Tara didn't move. Claire's eyes began to fill with tears, which was another shock. Her parents were the most stubborn, stalwart people she had ever known, and the only other time she had seen her mother cry was at Gran's funeral. It was disheartening.

"I'm sorry, Tara . . . for everything. I just . . . I didn't know how else to get you back here, and I was so horrible before you left. Please, forgive me." She wept, tears flowing freely from her eyes. In that moment, Tara's will to be right broke down, and she gently hugged her delicate mother. How had it come to this? How had she lost so much time already?

"I'm sorry, too," she whispered over and over again. She didn't dare ask again how much time her mother had left. It was evident that it couldn't be longer than a few months. As they took control of their emotions once again, the two women separated and wiped their eyes.

"You remember where your room is?" Claire asked.

"I do," Tara said.

"Well, why don't you get settled then, and wash up for tonight? The family is coming over for dinner to welcome you home."

Tara groaned.

"Can they come over next week? I'd like some time to prepare. Or run away." The comment was rewarded with a stern glance, one Tara was very used to. She had always said what was on her mind, which to her was being polite. Lying seemed rude, yet it was heartily accepted to keep the status quo. That never sat well with her, and it was one reason why she loved New England culture so much. If someone didn't like you, at least they were honest about it. Having grown up in a world of lies, that was like the nectar to her bee: refreshing.

"No, they cannot. I know things weren't ideal for you here growing up, Tara, but I think you'll be surprised at how much everyone misses you, how much they love you."

"No offense, Mom, but I have to call bullshit." After what they had done to destroy any semblance of childhood happiness she could have hoped for, she would not allow her mother to lie about a ridiculous concept like familial love. Her aunts, her father's parents — they had done nothing to confirm that what her mother said was true.

"No offense, Tara, but you should really learn the concept of accepting the mistakes of others and knowing that people can change."

"Well, I guess I have no choice but to find out, now do I?" she snapped, her bitterness returning. As she stared at her mother, she noticed that her blond hair was so much thinner. With that somber reminder, Tara conceded victory. Stubborn, the woman may be, but considering her condition, Tara found herself unable to keep up the fight. She grabbed a handle on each suitcase and lugged them upstairs to her room.

Interestingly enough, her room had been kept almost exactly as she left it. When she was younger, she was never into frills or childlike decorations. She wanted to escape. Although the space had changed with her parents' move a few years ago, the furniture was the same, displayed by her mother in a best approximation of how it had been. Maps of various countries lined the walls, and paintings of exotic locations she hoped to see one day hung between them. Her dresser was designed to look like a pile of suitcases, as was her bedside table. The window at the head of her bed looked directly into the house next door, not exactly the most scenic view for either party. Tara stared out at the neighboring windows, their blinds closed tight.

She plopped onto her bed and stared out into empty memories that battled with a bemusing present. Her father had shown the largest burst of emotion she had ever seen from him, his cool-as-a-cucumber shell cracked by the threat of losing his wife too soon. Tara struggled with how to proceed from here. Her anger toward this place and the people in it choked her in a vicelike grip, and yet . . .

To return to the belly of the beast only to see her mother suffering and her father in complete duress made her want to try. If she could somehow make her mother happy, or at least satisfied by having her there these last few months, maybe things would have a way of working out. A few errant tears escaped again. She had the feeling they were just the beginning.

It was time to face her past and try to learn how to forgive. She didn't know whether she had it in her. Gran's voice echoed in her mind.

Try to see past what's there and learn to understand it before blindly hating it.

As if that could be easily done. Tara fiercely ached for Gran; a cup of tea and a knitting project while she told her exactly what to do was just what she needed.

•••

Chapter Six

Hot water ran over Tara's head and shoulders, washing the grime of travel away. She stared out into her own mind, not fighting the flashes of memory anymore. What was the point?

Things were finally starting to go right.

Following Gran's advice, Tara had canvassed the community trying to find something that could help her get into college. She finally stopped in at the local library, and after listening to her tale, they graciously took her on as a page assistant. Although the library was no gem, it was staffed with kind and generous women, all of whom were happy to bestow their knowledge of the written word on Tara's eager ears.

She started immediately. On her first day, a lot of her time was spent shelving books and patching the extra-worn ones together, and she was given the project of preserving some old photographs in the library archive. The archivist in charge of the project noticed the gleam in Tara's eyes as she spoke of the preservation techniques, and before long she had herself a full-time assistant. Tara had finally found something that made sense to her, and it was all due to Gran. Having had a particularly wonderful day, Tara opted to stop in for tea to tell her all about it.

She pulled up the driveway and jogged happily through the garage, not bothering to kick off her shoes in her excitement.

"Gran!" she called out. Silence. That was strange. . . . Gran was always in the kitchen at this time of day. She strolled in that direction and then glanced around the empty room, confused.

"Gran?" she called out. All the doors were open. She peeked in every room, and nothing. Finally, she reached the master bedroom. *Maybe she was gardening and decided to take a shower,* Tara thought. She pushed the door wide open and walked in to see her Gran tucked in bed.

"Gran, what are you doing, you lazy bum? You hate naps," she chittered as she plopped on the bed and waited for her to wake up. She didn't move. Tara gently shook her arm.

"Gran, are you okay . . . ?" she asked, touching her face to feel her temperature. Her skin was cold. Tara looked down. Her chest was still. It took the seventeen-year-old girl less than five seconds to realize that her grandmother was dead.

"Gran!" she screamed, as though shouting at her would somehow jar her back to life. "No! Please, Gran. No, no, no . . ." She began to cry, and she stood up and stepped back from her grandmother's motionless body. She couldn't look away from her relaxed face. She looked as though she slept in peace. God, if only she could just be sleeping.

"What will I do without you?" she whispered. Finding the will to reach for the phone, she called her mother, unable to suppress her sobs. After relaying what had happened, Tara listened to her mother's firm voice instructing her to stay there until they arrived. The phone line was dead before she could even think to push the button and end the call. She gazed down at her grandmother's face again, and her own folded in grief. She had lost her one friend in the world.

Tara curled up next to her grandmother's body, not caring how morbid it might seem. She spent the better part of the half hour it took for her parents to arrive trying to bargain with God for her Gran's life back. They found her like that, sobbing and pleading with no one, and her father quickly took her into the other room.

"Are you fit to drive, Tara?" he asked, all business. Her father was a take-charge kind of man, and she often felt like his employee rather than his kid. She steeled herself and met his steady gaze, because she had to.

"Yes," she said without preamble.

"Good. I need you to go home and call your sister. Let her know what happened, and tell her to drive down from Greeley as soon as she can. We have to make arrangements."

Tara went into soldier mode, holding back her tears as she drove home as quickly as the speed limit would allow. It was like driving through a dense fog.

Her grandmother was gone. The one person who had made her life bearable . . . gone. It was like a black hole had opened up in her heart and begun to suck the rest of her in.

She reached home before realizing that she had traversed the distance. The phone call was made, and before she knew it, there Ali was, tears reddening her eyes. Whatever differences the girls had had growing up, their grandmother had been a constant in both their lives — a connector of sorts. Though the eldest was the golden child and the youngest was the outsider, the two embraced in the same grief.

"What are they going to do?" her sister asked as she wiped her eyes. In seeing her grief, Tara forced herself to be strong. She wiped her eyes forcefully.

"What do you think?" she asked, her anger flaring. "The funeral will be arranged, just like Grandpa's."

Ali took offense at her tone.

"You don't have to be a bitch about it, Tara. I loved her, too." Her tone revealed her jealousy that Tara was considered an equal in

Gran's eyes, if not slightly favored. Ali was used to being the favorite, and not being Gran's did not seem to be a sore spot until today. Tara stared at the ground, her expression vacant.

"That doesn't really matter now, does it?" Tara said bitterly. "I've got a few short months left, and then I'll be gone. She was my only reason to stay." She knew she was venturing into dicey territory. She was never encouraged to speak her mind in regard to her desperate need to escape.

"Your only reason?" Ali asked, her eyes wide. She had never understood Tara's emotional dissonance with her favorite state, the beautiful paradise that Tara had shunned since birth. And she would never grow to understand. Tara continued to stare off, her expression firm yet somehow lost.

"I will go, as soon as I can. I want you to be prepared for it."

"She would have wanted you to stay. She would have wanted you to fight your own prejudice against a concept of a world *you've* created for yourself!" Ali shouted. With the loss of a grandmother, this talk of losing a sister immediately after was almost just as painful. Nevertheless, Tara's expression did not change.

"Don't ask me to stay here, Ali. I've never belonged here like you have. Ever. Please," she begged, tears returning to her eyes as she forced herself to look back at her sister. Ali blinked for a moment, paralyzed by what her words implied. They stared at each other, exchanging an entire dialogue's worth of words without them needing to be said. Suddenly, Ali grabbed Tara fiercely and hugged her tight. Hot tears seeped into Tara's shoulder.

"I know, I know," Ali repeated over and over again, delirious in her own grief. "I'm so sorry, Tara. I wish it were different. I don't know why they favored me. I really don't." Tara pulled away and gave a feeble smile.

"It's okay. It's not your fault. I just have to go. I always have."

Ali collected herself and nodded. "I know," she said. Ali understood so little about her sister, but she did know that when she made up her mind, it was final. She would find any opportunity she could to be gone as soon as possible. It was her way, and it always had been. That had never stopped her from hoping desperately that somehow things could be different, that somehow Tara could feel the warm acceptance she herself had always encountered as a child.

Ali wasn't blind to the way her sister had been treated. When Christmases passed and she was given elaborate gifts while Tara breathed in the mothball scent of one of her aunt's old sweaters, she thought she should say something. When her grandparents complimented her hair and good looks and then cast glares at Tara, she pondered speaking up for her then, too. When it came down to it, she had been afraid to stand up for Tara, and now she was more or less gone. Regret filled her, mixing with grief in a wretched cocktail of emotions.

The front door opened then, and their father entered. Seeing their distress, he reached his arms out, and Ali collapsed into them as she cried. Tara was secretly glad it was Ali hugging him over her. She knew that she would have felt awkward in such an embrace. With Gran gone, there was nothing for her . . . no support, no love. As much as her parents had tried to be there, the bond they had with her sister would clearly get them through her own departure. It was time to go.

They learned shortly after that Gran had been hiding her cancer diagnosis for a short while, knowing that she barely had time to let anyone know anyway. Cancer was funny like that, the way it chose how short or long someone would suffer. Just hilarious.

Tara slid a plain black dress over her head and let it drape down over her body.

She felt numb, as if the one glowing sliver of light in her darkened world had been snuffed out.

The funeral passed in a blur of tears and devastation. Tara watched as the coffin was lowered into the earth, her grandmother becoming one with a planet she had always understood better than her. Her aunts and uncles on her mother's side stayed the requisite amount of time before departing back to their own lives. They never showed any interest in Tara's, so naturally, they had very little to say to her during the short ceremony. Tara was glad — she wasn't there for them. She wept openly and bitterly for her loss. The idea that she would have to find her own way struck home in those moments. She had already contacted a student advisor to find out how to graduate early. In a few short months, she would be gone.

She had seen enough loss in this place for her short lifetime. Boston was calling.

Tara made her way downstairs after an hour of staring down her every flaw in the mirror. She would not become the self-conscious girl they knew her to be and had created within her. She had taken extra care with her hair and even opted to put on makeup — something she would never normally do. It was clear that her relatives still had influence over her. As she made herself up to look her best, she condemned her reflection for letting them matter. She was an adult, a successful adult, and she could take on whatever little insults they threw at her.

Her mother was busy placing various food items in their proper place. It looked like a roast with mashed potatoes and fresh-baked rolls would be on the menu, much to Tara's delight. Tara's mother was always able to put a good meal together. The problem was always the familial company that came along with it. Spotting a bottle of red wine on the counter, Tara made her way over to it and took a look.

"Merlot. Nice . . .," she commented. Her mother pretended to be too busy with cooking to initiate conversation. Suddenly, that three-year gap began to present itself, and Tara was afraid of it. She hoped that somehow they could find lasting forgiveness before it was too late. Claire glanced at Tara before returning to mashing her potatoes.

"Well, I know it's your favorite," she said as she pounded away. Tara opened a few drawers before she found the bottle opener. She poured herself a healthy glass. At least being back as an adult meant that she could use alcohol to calm her nerves.

"Where's Dad?" Tara asked, glancing around as she took a seat at the kitchen table.

"He's smoking a cigar on the porch. You'd think he'd give it up, all things considered, but it soothes him," she said matter-of-factly. *No beating around the bush with this situation, then*, Tara mused. She nodded and continued to sip at her wine. She really did like a good merlot . . . even if, to her thinking, good meant four bucks at the liquor store. She was an archivist, after all, not a lawyer. And libraries didn't pay.

The front door opened and slammed shut, and the clucking of her aunts' voices rang in the air, poisoning it.

Here we go. Tara took a large gulp of wine. Like a tsunami, her family flooded into the room, and she found herself face-to-face with the familiar personalities of her youth. Aunt Jo and Aunt Marilyn came in first. Not surprising — they loved a grand entrance. Tara noticed the brittle texture of their bleached hair and their leathery skin that had soaked in sun for too many years. They were the quintessential suburban housewives. To Tara's amusement, she noticed that Marilyn's eyes darted straight toward the wine bottle before actually meeting hers.

"Hi, Tara!" she said, all smiles. Tara stood, as it was clear her aunt was rushing in for a hug. She smelled of designer perfume, and the scent lingered after she pulled away and Aunt Jo took her place. *Now this is different*, she thought. Her perfume had a slightly different scent, but Tara felt the same level of pretension. She did her best not to make the hugs awkward before her cousins strolled in behind them.

Her cousin Kennedy, whom Tara had babysat when Kennedy was a small child, had grown into a sleek, thin eighteen-year-old. She was her mother's daughter; she wore heavy eye makeup, but not enough to seem trashy or tasteless. Behind her was fourteen-year-old Josh, who had developed enough hormones to now tower over Tara, though his expression was painfully shy. He had been very outgoing as a child, she remembered.

Kennedy ran up next and pulled Tara into a fierce hug. Her words seemed to come out all at once, with no spaces for breath in between. "Oh my God I can't believe you're actually here we finally have the whole family together again!" she exclaimed.

Tara patted her back. She was a bit uncomfortable, as though hugging a stranger for the first time. She dug deep for her must-please-Dad-by-accepting-his-relatives smile. But the longer she looked at her cousin, she realized her smile was actually real. After all, the two kids had done nothing to warrant ill feelings — in fact, Tara had always been fond of the dynamic duo. She waved to Josh, who gave a small wave back with a smirk. Fourteen-year-olds never really liked to talk, and in this crowd, it was always particularly difficult to do so.

Tara went back to her glass of wine and watched her aunts each grab one for themselves, chattering the whole time about traffic and shopping and the price of gas. It seemed as though their repertoire of topics never ran dry. They continued in a never-ending cycle of mindless conversation amongst themselves, with Tara occasionally nodding as she poured herself her second glass of wine.

"So," Aunt Jo asked, "how is the East Coast? I hear it's horribly humid and the people are snobs."

"No more so than here, that's for sure," Tara blurted. And then she laughed. Did she seriously just say that? Did Jo get the reference? She seemed confused.

"What are you talking about, Tara? People here are wonderful
. . . so laid-back!"

Aunt Marilyn piped in with agreement. "Absolutely! Obviously,
Tara's just become a little too much like them. Don't you think?"

The two cackled at their own cleverness, and Tara felt her cheeks
burn. Wine quickly followed.

"Well, I suppose I'd rather be strange here and normal in a
world of sane, well-educated people," she spat out with a syrupy smile.
A very small voice in her head started whispering warnings, but she
didn't want to listen. She didn't want them to have control over every
conversation, not when she had achieved so much more than they
ever believed she could. They looked taken aback, but before they
could retort — and God knew what would be coming out about her
bland looks or terrible manners — the door opened again. This time,
Ali walked in with her husband and baby girls, one toddling alongside
her and the other sleeping in her carrier. All the bitterness of the
moment seeped away when she saw her two little nieces, whom she
had longed to pick up and hold for so long.

Tara rose and made her way to the door, ignoring her aunts
completely. Ali looked up and smiled broadly.

"Hey there, stranger," she said, struggling with diaper bags and
her infant. Tara grabbed a few of her mommy accessories and helped
her set them on the floor.

"Hey, yourself," she replied, relishing in the chance to hug her
sister.

"Has it broken out in a fight yet?" Ali whispered in her ear mid-
embrace. Tara barked out a laugh.

"Not yet, but the night's still young," she replied.

Ali rolled her eyes. "Uh-huh," she muttered as she bent down to
her eldest child, Madison.

"Have you said hi to Auntie Tara yet, Maddie?"

The child looked up and grinned.

"Tara!" she exclaimed, holding up her thin, little arms. "Up!"

Tara scooped up her niece and tossed her into the air for good measure, which won her a mirthful giggle. Pointing to Maddie's shirt, she said, "What color is this?"

Maddie focused hard on her shirt, her blue eyes in deep concentration as she pulled the fabric out from her tiny body with miniscule fingers. Then, she looked up with wide eyes and exclaimed, "Lellow!" with a smile full of growing teeth. Tara laughed.

"That's right!" she exclaimed, and she carried the child into the kitchen. Ali put her youngest, Emily, on the kitchen table and took a breath.

"Whew! There's no workout like a motherhood workout," she exclaimed, heading to the fridge for a glass of water. Madison clung to Tara as she took in everyone in the room, and her eyes settled on Kennedy.

"Kendy!" she squealed, squirming to be put down in order to run to her next favorite person. Although Tara hadn't been in Colorado, she did know how short Maddie's two-year-old attention span was. She set her down and watched her plummet over to her cousin, who settled the child firmly in her lap and continued conversing with Marilyn. Something about shoes. Tara reclaimed her wine and realized suddenly that she was on the verge of drunk. But somehow, not drinking did not seem like a feasible option, so she continued in her endeavor to numb herself enough from the pain of being home with these people who had alienated her for so long and now expected her to act as though they were all best friends.

Her father had come in from smoking his cigar and was fixing himself a Maker's on the rocks in a short glass. Glancing at the bottle of wine and then at Tara, he made a cautionary face but said nothing. She flashed a toothy smile at him, her teeth likely a radiant shade of purple, refusing to acknowledge his warning in any way. He swirled the ice around in his glass with a finger before making his way to the living room. Ali's husband, Harold, and Josh soon followed, and the three of them found a sporting event on TV to rescue them from the inane conversations taking place in the kitchen. Lucky bastards.

Tara asked her mother what she could do to help but was waved off. So she walked over to Ali, who was removing Emily from her car seat.

"Would you like to hold her?" Ali asked, shifting the baby into a more comfortable position.

"Yeah, sure," Tara said. She took her newborn niece gently to hold her for the first time. The little girl squirmed to get comfortable again, unfamiliar with being outside the comfortable womb. One eyelid cracked open, and Emily looked at Tara, accepting the new person holding her. Her face settled into something that resembled a smile but was more likely a poop. Still, Tara clung to this second born, hoping against hope that she would have a better time here with these people than she ever had.

A wave of protectiveness surged through Tara, and she held her little niece tight. She'd be damned if this helpless child were forced to succumb to her same fate.

"Tara! Jesus, have you gone deaf?" Ah, Aunt Jo. Tara looked up to the faces of her aunts and cousin. Her sister had gone to wash off some form of baby goo from her clothing.

"I'm sorry, what?" she asked, smirking. These people weren't used to being ignored. . . . Maybe that's why they were so loud.

"Is that the first time you've seen Emily?" Aunt Jo asked again. *What a hard life to have someone not hear your questions*, Tara thought.

She decided to attempt her Dad's excellent skill of speaking as little as possible. "In person, yes," she replied. Her aunts displayed the same look of brittle judgment they always wore whenever she replied to what they said.

"Well, it must be nice to be home with family again. It's about time you understood how important it is to have your family close," Aunt Marilyn piped in.

"It would be so much easier to value family if they actually gave two shits about me," Tara threw out, her heart pounding. She had never dared confront her aunts. What was she doing?

"That's enough, Tara. Dinner's ready, and I won't have spats over my roast," her mother announced. Tara caught the secret look that passed between her aunts, which didn't need translation.

Everyone obeyed her mother and went to grab plates. That was new; these women never listened to anyone, yet they had obeyed her mother with deference. Claire had never really been defiant with them either, and yet here she was commanding them as though she were the general and they her troops. Tara made it a point to place herself far away from her aunts for the rest of the evening and instead caught up with her cousins, though Kennedy looked at her with some trepidation. Tara imagined she had never seen another person say such a thing about family — apparently, everyone loved each other dearly while she was away. Imagine that.

As the evening wore down, Ali and Tara washed the dishes while everyone else enjoyed each other's company in the living room. Tara watched as her mother's constitution grew weaker and her gaze became distant. Her father's keen eye took notice of this as well, and he made the excuse of being old and tired as a means of getting the family to depart. She gave a wan smile from the kitchen, hoping her aunts wouldn't be confrontational. As always, this was too much to ask.

Both aunts approached her, and suddenly she was cornered. Ali stood by awkwardly drying the last few dishes wish a moist towel.

"I don't know what pity-party sob story you've created for yourself, Tara," Marilyn spat, "but your mother is dying. Maybe you could stop making this about you for once, okay?"

Tara glared into her aunt's aging eyes but said nothing. Why fuel their fire? When someone was so good at tearing others down, words of defense were their ammunition. Finally, she said, "I believe my father was politely trying to kick you out of our house."

Before they could turn, a retort arrived.

"By the way — Jo? Marilyn? You're never too old to start minding your own fucking business. This is my family, and you have no place here," she said, feeling slightly triumphant. They were stunned. They said nothing but mumbled about what a bitch she was before turning away and making their much-anticipated exit.

"That was foolish," Ali said with worry in her eyes. "They're Dad's sisters. They have his ear in a way we will never have."

"Someone needs to stand up to them, Ali. It can't be you — they like you too much. Let it be someone they could never stand."

Ali frowned and returned to her dishes. Maddie was beginning to throw a temper tantrum, which was the signal for Ali to start packing their bags. They all soon departed, and quiet was brought into the house again. Tara sat at the kitchen table and put her head in her hands. She was surprised when she felt a pair of hands begin to massage her shoulders.

"I never blamed you for leaving, Tara. Not really," Claire said softly as she pushed in small circles around her upper back and neck.

Tara closed her eyes. Tears brimmed at the edges.

"Really?" she asked, feeling completely vulnerable again. God, she hated it here. She hated who she was and who she returned to being when she came back. Did everyone have to look at her like she was crazy? Her mother began to run her fingers through her hair, her touch soothing her sadness while also making her tears flow heavier. There was so much grief that she had left behind for so long.

"You think I wanted to be left alone with those psychos?" she asked bluntly. Tara turned around in surprise.

"But all that spouting about family and my responsibility . . . what was that?"

"It was me being an idiot and using the wrong technique to try and get you to stay. I wanted you to stay so I could have someone to fight them at their own game. You've always been a lot stronger than you think, Tara."

Tara blinked, and her tears dissolved as shock replaced sadness. This whole time . . . had her mother really been hiding so much for so long? She searched her eyes wondering just who this woman was standing above her.

"Maybe now . . .," Tara said, doubt coloring her words. She was never brave as a child — it showed in the way her aunts bullied her while pampering her sister. She was clearly an easy target.

"Maybe always," Claire said as she resumed her massage of Tara's head. She had always done this when Tara was upset. Somehow it had always managed to ease her worries. It was amazing how a mother's touch had that power.

"I wish that we had been more honest with each other," Tara sniffed. This moment gave her pause. She dwelled on the impending loss of the woman who had given her life. It was so tragic, Tara thought, how death seemed to be the only way to get people to treat each other how they ought to. Why hadn't she had that wisdom sooner?

"I wish that, too, baby. I wish I had taken your side more than I did. I wish I'd had the strength to defend you when you needed it. Only Gran could do that. . . . She was a lot braver than me."

"I think you're pretty brave," Tara whispered. They fell into thoughtful silence then, and when Tara could feel her mother's touch softening, she stood and hugged her and made her own excuses about needing to get to bed. Claire would never admit to needing her own time to heal and recover, no matter how bad she looked.

As Claire left the kitchen and headed to bed, Tara stared after her, her mind reeling.

Did her mother regret not standing up for her? Had she really seen the way Tara had been treated and been too scared to do anything about it?

Her mind whirled with questions and memories as she reconsidered her life from a different point of view.

Perhaps there was more she had to learn from being back home than she realized.

•••

Chapter Seven

Tara brushed the stain of red wine from her teeth before rummaging through her suitcase for a pair of comfortable pajamas. It hit her that this was where she would be staying with no end in sight. With a heavy sigh, she pulled back the decorative comforter her mother had found on sale a few years back, leaned over to turn off the bedside lamp, and settled under the freshly washed sheets.

Tara stared at the dark ceiling trying to wrap her head around the fact that her mother had just admitted she knows her aunts are terrible. As the alcohol buzzed through her veins, she drifted off to sleep, her nightmares already prepped to torture her once more.

•

The family was spending Easter at Grandma Eve's house, as usual. Marilyn and Jo, ever the dutiful wives, had prepared a wide variety of food, ranging from ham to potatoes to fresh bread to another form of ham. It was Easter, after all, and everyone loved ham.

In her usual attempt to fade into the background, Tara sat downstairs by the large stone fireplace. The house was brown — brown paint, brown carpets, brown countertops. Only the fireplace, with its gray stone and heavy black iron doors, stood out. No one came to the basement very often anymore, and it had become a small sanctuary for when Tara finally got sick of the inane conversation between her relatives.

Since Gran's death, she had wasted no time keeping her mind occupied. She'd taken up running, and her body had slimmed down considerably in the past few months. Beyond this, her appetite was curbed, making her frame almost too thin. One of her friends began calling her Skeletor, but Tara was taking an unhealthy pride in her new figure. Her aunts glared at her with a new emotion, which Tara soon realized was jealousy. She had something they had lost — their youthful figures — and for the first time, they couldn't hide it from her. It was a small victory, but she relished in it.

She had been accepted to college in Boston and begun packing her things up for an early summer departure right after graduation. Somehow, she had managed to convince her mother that getting a job over the summer would help her acclimate to the region. Claire had been vacant from her life since the loss of Gran, her usual fire extinguished. Had Tara not been in such a rush to escape, she might have been more worried.

Tara was interrupted from her book by the sound of someone clearing their throat. She looked up to see Sam, Aunt Marilyn's husband, watching her from the bottom of the stairs with a strange glint in his eyes. Sam was a doctor, and when he wasn't working or complaining about how much money his wife spent, he was drinking or working out. Obsessed with maintaining a youthful countenance, he tanned to the extent of turning his skin orange and exercised hours a day to make up for the calories imbibed on boozy vacations. A cruise or a trip to Vegas was worked into each month, so this wonderful drunken form of his personality came out fairly often.

Sam was kinder to Tara than most others. He was always particularly funny while drunk, and as a child Tara never knew the difference. Fun was fun, and she clung to it. Now, though, his behavior was getting more and more out of control, to the point where the family wouldn't bring him out if they were celebrating something.

He began to hit on waitresses overtly, or really any female who came into his path with the right figure. It was disconcerting.

"What are you doing down here, Tara?" he asked, his words slurring slightly.

"Just reading," she replied. Unfortunately, that did not deter him, and he walked over to sit beside her, a little too close. She could smell the whiskey on his breath and leaned away. He leaned in, looking at her book.

"Whatcha reading?" His breath was hot in her face, bitter with drink.

"*The Grapes of Wrath*," she said, becoming wary. No one in her family, not even Sam, showed an interest in her intellectual pursuits. Characteristically, he scrunched his nose up in distaste.

"Isn't that depressing?" he asked, slowly pulling the book out of her hands and setting it down beside him. He leaned in toward her and placed a hand on her knee, gliding his fingertips up her thigh. She shot up and took a few steps away. Sam remained seated.

"What are you doing?!" she asked, shocked. He just looked up at her, his glassy eyes amused.

"We could do it, you know. No one would know."

"Are you out of your fucking mind?" she hissed. "We're related!" The one relative she had somewhat liked had just flashed his true colors. Her heart was racing; her mind was reeling with disgust and crushing disappointment. Sam was supposed to be on her side! She was supposed to trust him.

"Not by blood," he threw back with a laugh. That much was true — not that it should matter. She stood there evaluating whether or not he would jump at her if she were to try to pass him to get to the stairs. It seemed he was drunk enough to be thrown off balance. She made a run for it, and a rush of relief hit her once she saw he made no move to follow. She began taking the stairs two at a time. Her family would never believe her if she were to tell them what had just happened, and her aunts' verbal torture would only worsen. *Just a few short weeks to go before the escape*, she thought, fighting back tears.

"Hey, you forgot your book!" Uncle Sam yelled up, as if nothing were amiss. In that moment, she was so grateful for her decision to drive separately. She grabbed her purse from the kitchen and mumbled something about not feeling well to her mother before scurrying out of that house. If she were lucky, she would never have to see it again.

Of course, luck was never something Tara had particularly excelled at.

•

Tara bolted upright, a cold sheen of sweat glistening on her forehead. She glanced around the room and let out a breath.

It took two days for Tara to start going completely out of her mind. With nothing to occupy her time except watching her mother plant in the garden and her father tap away at his computer in his office, she found some crappy TV to watch and stared out over the rooftops at the towering mountains. Neither of these activities occupied her for very long, and Tara once again found herself being drawn into arguments with her mother.

"Stop moping around, Tara. You're upsetting the chi," Claire chastised from the kitchen, where her thin hands were tossing around a glob of cookie dough to bake sugar cookies for Maddie.

Tara allowed her eyes to refocus, having stared off into some unknown place. Maybe if she stared off long enough, she could move time and space and find herself back at her apartment in Boston. Sadly, that theory did not seem to be working. Hefting herself up from the sofa, Tara padded over to the kitchen and reached for a bottle of merlot.

"You know, it's only four in the afternoon," her mother said, glancing over with a critical look in her eyes. Tara ignored her and instead pulled out a wine glass, released the cork with a satisfying *pop*, and poured a healthy amount.

"It's five o'clock where it matters," she said with a false smile and a salute with her glass.

"I always thought you drank too much once you left. College ended a while ago, Tara. There's no need to pretend like it hasn't."

"Actually, if this were college, I'd be playing beer pong with cheap beer, not enjoying an adult glass of wine. But I appreciate your concern."

More silence ensued, broken only when her father came in to steal a chunk of cookie dough and kiss her mother on the forehead before going back to his office.

Tara took another sip.

"When can we expect Satan's minions back?" she asked dryly. She knew that the other night was just the beginning of a long series of battles she would have with her aunts. They wouldn't be getting off easy with their barbs ever again. Her comment elicited a critical look from Claire.

"Regardless of how they are, they are still your relatives. You shouldn't talk about them like that," she sniffed.

Guess the heart-to-heart of night one was irrelevant, Tara thought ruefully. Unable to repress her anger, she spit out a retort.

"You mean like how they never say anything rude?"

"You need to be the better person," Claire stated. She threw the cookie dough onto the counter a little firmer than necessary. Tara stared at her. It was then something occurred to her . . . that her mother might actually be coaching herself. *Be the better person.* Was that how she had dealt with the underhanded comments all these years?

"I think you should start looking for a job," Claire added.

"What?" Tara asked, surprised.

"You heard me. A job. Something to keep you from becoming a drunk."

"I am not a drunk," Tara said, setting her glass down. Claire eyed her with what looked to be a spark of amusement. Tara narrowed her eyes and said, "And what exactly do you propose I do to while away the hours here, in my favoritest of places?"

Claire waved a hand nonchalantly. "Oh, I don't know. I'm sure you'll figure something out."

"Mmhmm," Tara mumbled, now acutely aware that her mother was up to something, which usually ended badly.

"Also, we're doing family dinner at Grandma Eve's tonight."

"Well, you have fun with that."

Claire frowned. "Tara, I will not fight you on this at every turn. It's important that you start to see beyond your anger and try to learn to forgive."

"Ok. . . . I forgive them. But, boy, do I feel sick. . . . Probably going to need bed rest tonight . . ."

"We'll be leaving at six. You might want to sober up by then."

The cookie dough had been roughly rolled out, and Claire was in the process of cutting it into circular pieces. Tara knew from experience that those little circles would turn into smiley faces, moons and various Picasso-looking objects by the end of the evening. Her mother enjoyed making creative cookies, even if she wasn't particularly artistic about it.

Tara sat for a minute and stared at her mother, who continued to ignore her gaze. She then picked up her glass and made her way toward the stairs. *Just like old times — holing up in my room to prepare for the worst,* she thought. She set her glass down on her wooden bedside table, plopped onto her bed, and pulled out her cell phone.

Feeling morose, Tara scanned her contact list for someone who could console her. Cris's name came up first. Tara clicked on it and hit Call as she reached again for her wine glass to take a sip.

"Are you drinking?" was all Cris said when she answered the phone.

"How could you guess?" Tara asked wryly.

"Because you're in Littleton, Colorado, and it's been three days since I've heard from you. What's up?"

Tara sat up and wrapped her arms around her knees, careful to not spill on her bedspread. She was glad to hear a voice from home.

"It's pretty bad here, Cris," she said grimly. She explained how the meeting with her mother first went, how frail her mother now looked, and how she tried to keep others from seeing that she was in pain. When Tara got to the part about her spat with her aunts, Cris couldn't help but cheer.

"I can't believe you said that! That's amazing!"

Tara's laugh was laced with bitterness. "Yeah, well, I won't be making anymore friends here. That's for sure."

"Who needs 'em? You hang in there and spend as much time as you can with your mother, Tara. If she's as sick as you say, that seems like the best thing to do. Don't let the others distract you."

"You're right. I didn't mention that she totally told me she wishes she'd stood up for me more."

"You're kidding. . . . Why didn't she?"

Tara stared into the bottom of her glass. She was still asking herself the same question.

"I don't know, but I think there's more to my past and my mother than I realized. Maybe it'll be good to get that resolved."

"Now you're talking. Silver linings are important! Try to focus on that, and dodge as many dumb comments from your relatives as you can. You're there to be there for your mother. Don't bother with anyone else's crap."

Tara sighed. "You're right. Thank you for being the voice of reason."

"Anytime! That's what I'm here for: perfect logic and emotional stability," she said with a chuckle.

"Uh-huh. So how's the guy you're with? Still making weird orgasm noises?"

"Naw, he's gotten better. I'm just trying not to freak out about the fact that he's nice and treats me well. I'll probably bolt if he calls today. . . . We just saw each other last night!"

The beacon of emotional stability . . . right . . ., Tara thought.

"Well, I hope things work out however you want them to."

"Thanks!" Cris replied cheerfully. "I'll let you know when I figure out what that is, and if I still want it after I decide that I want it."

"You are ever the rational, unwavering, emotionally stable one, my friend," Tara said with a laugh.

"You know me! Anyway, we're about to head out. . . . Shenanigans is doing dollar-beer night and trivia. It's pretty much going to be the best thing ever."

"Sounds like it," Tara replied, her mood dimming with the realization that she would be spending the evening fighting off her aunts rather than laughing in the company of friends.

"Good luck, and text me if you need to talk, okay?"

Tara said she would and ended the call. Talking about men had brought to mind a particular happy-go-lucky bar friend who she hadn't really thought about since arriving at her parents' house. She wondered just how sincere he was when he told her to text him. No one liked to be pressured by the needy. It was stressful and unattractive. Would she come off that way texting so soon?

Well, what the hell? He did say he'd be my one Colorado friend, she reasoned.

Scrolling through her phone again, she slid her finger across the screen and stopped at Tom Sanders. She clicked on his name to type a text message and then paused, unsure of how to begin. After a minute of thought and evaluation, she made her decision, typed it in, and hit send.

So, how's life on the farm?

Not too forward . . . vague enough that he could ignore it and not feel bad, and she wouldn't feel slighted. She slid her phone back onto the table and picked up her glass only to discover that it was empty.

She deliberated for a short while whether or not to get another and then decided against it. The drunker she was, the more difficult it would be to spar with her family. It was something she could not risk, since she knew how talented they were. A second later, her phone buzzed.

Oh, you know. Planting plants and selling things to stay alive. I'm so glad to hear from you! How's family life? Much better than you expected?

Tara smiled, despite herself. He was certainly one of the most pleasant people she had ever met. However, keeping herself distant was the only way to keep him from getting too close, she decided. No use in starting something that would never amount to anything, after all. She typed her reply, grinning as she did.

Planting plants must be particularly pleasant. Family life is as expected. . . . If no further texts received, just know the bloodsuckers have made me one of their own and I shall be a danger to society.

She chucked the phone back onto the bed and made her way to the bathroom to take a shower. She tried to focus on the relaxing droplets of warm water on her skin, but her muscles remained taught with dread. Here, in Littleton, there was always dread. . . . It seeped under her skin. Stepping from the shower, she shivered as she wrapped a towel around her body and brushed her hair before heading back to the bedroom, where her phone blinked invitingly. A jolt of excitement shot up through her gut . . . a bad sign. Still, she ignored the warning voice in her head — the one everyone ignores when they want to flirt unabashedly — and scooped up her cell to read his message.

Planting parsnips is particularly pleasing to me. Also, this is wonderful news, as I can bring my vampire rehabilitation serum and bring you back to life.

Ah, so he wanted to be the rescuer, did he? That was probably already going too far. Tara sent out a quick and final *"good to know"* before getting ready for the evening. She was worried that Tom Sanders was the kind of man who could make her laugh for the rest of her life. . . . And when the time came to leave, that would just make it all the more difficult.

She would not contact him again. That was that.

Tara took another glance in the mirror, thoughts of Tom fading as her childhood memories invaded. She wondered how long it would take to suppress them again once she was gone. This time, she remembered Grandma Eve's house, a place she hoped never to step foot in again.

Christmas Eve was passing much as it usually did. The family came together to play a game in the living room, almost always charades, and to gather around the withering husk that was her grandfather. Grandpa Jon sat hunched, his prosthetic legs hanging from his yellowing knees. His illness was getting worse, and the more time that passed, the harder it became to ignore it.

Still, the Kingston family was exceptionally talented at looking the other way. Tara's Uncle Paul sat silently in the corner. He had never been particularly social, but Tara liked him. While most family members ignored her or berated her, Uncle Paul actually praised her for her achievements. Glancing over at him now, she began to feel a strange buzzing in her ears.

The man had been lost since his wife's death. He was short and balding and had lacked self-confidence since birth. Her father did his best to protect his brother from bullying and other forms of abuse, but he wasn't able to be there every time. Uncle Paul rarely made eye contact, and if he did, he didn't hold the gaze for more than an instant. When he was younger, he was prone to outbursts, and Grandma Eve was forced to restrain him a few times.

Tonight, Tara felt a cold chill run down her spine when she looked at him. Something was wrong. Surely, others could tell, too, but no one was saying anything about it. Her aunts, who had always resented having a troll for a brother (as they deemed him), spoke to him very little to begin with. Still, he was required to come to family events — there was a protocol to follow, after all.

So everyone openly ignored him and left him to sit alone. Tara decided to go downstairs and start watching a movie, her young cousin Kennedy always two steps behind her. For some reason, Kennedy had always taken a liking to Tara, which she found strange given the child's mother's attitude toward her. But she was content to have someone around who actually liked her, so she didn't question it. She led the little girl downstairs. They were snuggled under a blanket for a while before Tara heard the shouting.

Curious, she gently placed the sleeping little girl flat on the couch and made her way toward the staircase. She didn't make it far before Claire came barreling down the stairs with Ali, who looked pale.

"What's going on?" Tara asked.

"Nothing," her mother said quickly, pulling her and Ali to the couch. "Let's just watch this movie while your father takes care of it."

"Takes care of what?"

Claire paused.

Finally, she said, "Your uncle was just found hanging in Grandma's closet. Dad is trying to resuscitate him."

"What?!"

"Just stay down here, Tara. We don't need to alarm Kennedy, and we'd only be in the way."

Tara stared at the stairs. She knew nothing about CPR or how to help someone who had suffocated himself. She was helpless. She sat and waited with her mother and sister, staring blankly at the uplifting holiday movie that had been entertaining just moments before. After what seemed like ages, her father slowly came down the stairs, his face somber.

"What happened?" Tara asked. Claire had tried to get the girls to lie down and sleep, but neither of them had been willing or able to do so. Her father leaned his back against the gray stone of the fireplace and put his head in his hands.

"The ambulance took him away. We'll have to deal with the body in the morning and make arrangements," he said.

Claire began to cry softly, holding Ali close. Tara sat alone on an opposite sofa, staring at her father in disbelief. Finally, she asked, "So, what do we do? Go home?"

Her uncle had just killed himself on Christmas Eve while the family partied in the other room. Surely, going home to spend a quiet evening was the appropriate thing to do?

"No," her father said, raising his head to pierce her with a stare. "We will go on as usual. The kids shouldn't know that anything is wrong."

"Are you serious? We're just going to go on like nothing happened?" Tara asked. Protecting the children was one thing, but pretending that this traumatic event never occurred was quite another.

"That's enough, Tara," her father said, his voice a steel rod of discipline. After staring at him for a moment, she rose and made her way up the stairs. Her aunts were drinking in the kitchen, their usual response to anything happening. Tara hung back in the hallway and listened.

"He always was a sad little man," she heard Aunt Marilyn profess.

"I can't believe he did this on Christmas Eve. I just can't believe he would do that to us!" Aunt Jo added.

Unable to listen to any more, Tara turned to find her grandmother sitting in the living room, staring straight ahead, her eyes glazed over. Her short white curls seemed to droop around her face. Her slumped back revealed a slight hunch. Afraid that she might have done something to herself, Tara hurried over.

"Grandma?" she said softly, gently shaking her shoulder. This jarred the woman out of her reverie, and she shook Tara's hand off her shoulder.

"I'm fine," she hissed. She stood, the hump on her back even more pronounced than usual, and walked slowly to her bedroom. Tara stared as she realized her grandmother was shuffling to the room in which her son had just killed himself. Were they really that devoted to business as usual? Tara assumed that her grandfather had been put to bed somewhere, as he was nowhere in sight. She watched Grandma Eve hobble down the hall to her bedroom and close the door softly behind her.

Not knowing what else to do, Tara made her way back downstairs, where she found her parents asleep on the floor, her sister curled up on one couch and Kennedy spread out on the other. Tara found another spot on the floor and lay on her back, convinced that she would be awake until they were permitted to leave sometime the next day.

Hours later, she heard voices from somewhere far away.

"Tara, time to get up," Claire whispered. Tara opened one eye and then the other. Her mother's smiling face hovered above her.

"Santa came!" she said in a hushed tone. Slowly, Tara sat up. There beneath the fake silver-limbed Christmas tree sat an enormous pile of presents. Her aunts, uncles, cousins, and grandparents were all downstairs, the picture of good cheer.

"Finally, Tara," Aunt Marilyn threw out. "Let's get this started!"

Taking the cue, Tara's father took his place as the official hander-outer of presents, and Christmas morning went on as normal. The one thing missing was Uncle Paul.

He was not mentioned again for the rest of the day, until her father took Grandma Eve to the hospital to deal with his remains. Tara continued to sit numb with disbelief, mourning silently for the other unwanted family member who was lost and not grieved.

She wondered how quickly they would have opened presents had she died instead.

Chapter Eight

They pulled up to the old brown house, and her father parked in his usual spot in the driveway. The structure of all the houses in this neighborhood was more unique, though all were those same shades of brown. Tara grabbed the bag of cookies, and the three of them made their way through the small unkempt gardens surrounding the pathway to the front door.

A bare pear tree stood to their left. Mint plants that were planted years before and never stopped growing dominated to the right. Tara bent down and picked a sprig, crushing it between her fingers and breathing in the refreshing, piercing scent. When she was younger, she would wander around the outside of the house alone chewing on mint leaves.

Her father led the way inside. Reluctantly, Tara followed behind her mother, who stopped and gave her hand a quick squeeze and a reassuring smile. Tara winced back in an attempt to reciprocate the gesture. She hadn't been in this house in years. It still had the old, musty smell of unwashed surfaces and rugs, the same brown on brown on brown style. Whoever thought that was a good decorative theme? They made their way into the kitchen. It was large and spacious and centered around a big island.

Her aunts stood with their glasses of wine in hand, gossiping madly about something Tara was sure she didn't care about in the slightest. At their entry, all eyes came their way, and Tara noticed the brief flicker of resentment that passed between her aunts before they pasted on their smiles and greeted her family. Ali and Harold were feeding the babies at the kitchen table. When Maddie saw Tara, she began bouncing excitedly in her chair.

"Tara! Tara! Tara! Yay!" she cheered. Tara smiled back and waved to her niece, who wiggled her wrist up and down in a wave. Kennedy hopped off the chair and ran to her side and slipped her arm through Tara's.

"Hey, Tar-Tar!" she said smoothly, proud of her new nickname. Tara smirked.

"Tar-Tar?"

"Yeah! That's what you get to be called now. You can call me Kens," she replied. It was clear she was excited to have a new relationship with her long-absent cousin. Tara smiled — one of her first genuine smiles since arriving. After all, Kennedy was in no way responsible for the actions of Tara's parents, and she clearly had no idea what had transpired during Tara's childhood. Tara longed to share the girl's enthusiasm for their family . . . misguided as it was.

"Sounds like a plan, Kens." They made their way to the kitchen table and took the last two seats, Kennedy narrowly dodging a carrot thrown by Madison.

"Maddie, please do *not* throw your food at Kennedy," Ali said. The young child looked at her with a gleam in her eye, and it was clear that although she understood, she would ignore such warnings in the very near future. She made eye contact with Tara, and Tara winked at her young niece before she once again became interested in her tiny, colorful plate.

Tara sat down at the small round table she had sat at so many times before: the table where her grandfather reminded her of how ugly she was, the very same place her aunt remarked on her freakishly

large arms and moustache. Tara was barely thirteen then. She begged
her mother to get her face waxed as a result, and her mother
complied without argument. This had proven their point quite well —
she was an ugly child with no potential.

Tara took a deep breath, trying to push down the anger that
continued to rise up when she was faced with a memory. Repressing
them had done nothing but make her resentment fresher, like an
open cut rather than a scab or a scar.

"I bet it feels so cool to be back in this house!" Kennedy said, all
aglow with youth and happiness. Tara put on a good face and
pretended nothing was wrong. Still, her return had brought with it a
new level of courage. She would not lie and pretend everything was
okay anymore.

"Not really," she said with a small smile. "I actually hated this
house growing up."

Kennedy looked at her in confusion. "Seriously?" she asked, her
voice laced with incredulity. "This house has so many fun places to
hide and explore. . . . I always thought it was an adventure!"

"Mmhmm," was all Tara could say. How could she tell her young
cousin how awful her brother was? How he tortured her and Ali?
How her grandmother never cared? It was obvious that Kennedy was
very fond of her family unit, even if it did bicker at a nearly constant
rate.

"Did you like it here, Ali?" Kennedy asked. Ali was in the
process of wiping various colors of vegetable goo off of her eldest
child's face. She glanced briefly at Tara before looking back at
Kennedy, obviously unsure of how to answer.

"I could see how it could be a fun place," she offered
diplomatically. *Very well-played, sister,* Tara thought.

Kennedy nodded, satisfied. As long as someone agreed with her,
she seemed content to move on with the conversation. She turned to
her mother.

"Mom, when is dinner going to be ready?" Kennedy asked Marilyn. Marilyn took a sip of wine and glanced over at Grandma Eve, who was hunched over a large pot of stew, stirring it ever so slowly.

"Mom? You going to be finishing that any time soon?" Marilyn asked. Grandma Eve looked up with disdain in her eyes before masking it with matronly affection.

"Twenty more minutes, babies. I know, I know. I'm just an old lady now. . . . It's not so easy being seventy-two, you know . . .," she mumbled.

Tara watched as her father took the guilt-laced hint and took the wooden spoon from his mother's withered hand to stir the soup. Tara found herself faced with twenty minutes of potentially having to force civil conversation with her aunts, an unsavory thought, so she rose from the table as if to head to the bathroom.

Instead, she ambled down the long hall to her grandmother's bedroom. She knew exactly what memory she would find in there. It was swirling like a dark cloud, choking her with bitterness and disgust. She breathed in the scent of her broken youth, the childhood that was stolen from her without apology or acknowledgment. How could she learn to forgive these people, as Gran had often advised? As her mother had advised? The russet-colored double doors of Eve's bedroom were open, as always. The decades-old carpet was tattered. The bed that Tara's grandfather died in still stood against the back wall, the blankets the very same. She had always been a little grossed out that Grandma Eve had neglected to change anything in their room since that night. She hoped that at least the bedding had been washed, as her grandfather had literally rotted to death, spent his final days having his gaping bedsore cleaned in that very place.

She didn't come back here for this memory, though. She paused, looking down at the floor. Steeling her nerves, she reminded herself that she was not the kind of Kingston who avoided what was. Quickly, she looked up at her grandma's open closet.

There were just clothes — old, musty clothes covering the memory and storing it away. Tara stared at this unremarkable spot. She was amazed that a life could have been lost and erased so easily. Her eyes filled with tears, and she allowed a few to fall as she finally, after all these years, grieved for the uncle who had lost his will to live on a Christmas Eve she could never forget.

"I'm so sorry, Uncle Paul," she whispered, running her hand delicately along a long, dingy sleeve. In this moment, she had never felt closer to anyone than the ghost of her dead uncle . . . a man she barely knew.

"Tara?"

She turned at the high-pitched sound of her niece's voice. Maddie looked excited, as though she had caught her during a game of hide-and-seek. Tara recovered from her flashback, put her hands over her eyes, and quickly shifted them to the side, shouting, "Boo!" Maddie squealed in delight and began tottering back toward the kitchen. Taking a deep breath, Tara wiped her eyes lightly and stepped into the hall. Her sister was there waiting, Maddie giggling in her arms.

"Dinner's ready," was all Ali said before flipping Maddie up in her arms and giving her a raspberry, ensuing in more of Maddie's delighted laughter. Tara secretly hoped she would always have cause to be so joyful. She followed them back into the kitchen, ready for a glass of wine. Clear mind be damned . . . there was no way to survive this night without alcohol.

She reached for a bottle of merlot, poured a healthy glass, and took a large gulp in an attempt to clear her mind of the cobwebs of the past.

"Somebody is a healthy drinker," Aunt Jo remarked with a sneer.

"It all runs in the family, alchie," she shot back with a snake-like grin. She lifted her glass in a mock toast.

"Soup's on," her father announced in his own attempt to break the tension with food. Grandma Eve slowly took a place at the table.

Tara's father scooped out a healthy ladleful of piping-hot stew for her and buttered a slice of French bread, while everyone else helped themselves.

The rest of the meal went smooth enough. Having the babies nearby as a constant distraction kept the sharks at bay, and Tara managed to slip into her old persona of nonexistence. They placed Emily in a baby swing by her feet, so she kept a steady eye on the blushing young child. When she became fussy, Tara lifted her up and cradled her close. Tara felt a rush of warmth shoot through her, and she marveled at how easy it was to fall in love with babies. But she then frowned, thinking about what life would be like for Emily here.

What if she didn't like makeup? Or shopping? Would they alienate her, too? Would she be ignored in favor of her rambunctious older sister? *You're projecting,* she reminded herself. It wasn't fair to assume Emily would go through the same experience of being an outsider in her own family. Then again, if Tara were to stay, she could protect her from such a thing ever happening . . .

No, no. That's silly. Pushing that thought away, she brought her mind back to the room, where her aunts had begun clearing the table and washing dishes. Grandma Eve continued to sit hunched over, but now she stared openly at Tara with an unreadable expression.

"Holding a child suits you, Tara," Grandma Eve said. Tara blinked. Was that a compliment? At this table?

"Um, thanks," she replied.

"When can we expect some babies from you, young lady?" she asked with a small smile. Was this . . . friendliness? Warmth? The twilight zone? Tara laughed out of sheer discomfort and the awkwardness of the question itself.

"Not any time soon, I'd wager," she replied. In order to have children, one must have a partner. . . . or at least Tara wanted one. Her thoughts flashed to Tom, and she shooed them away as quickly as possible. Tom Sanders was not an option, no matter how cute his face was, or how kind and wonderful he was. Not happening.

"As someone who has no concept of the importance of family, that's not really surprising," Aunt Marilyn shot back. Tara felt her body tense, and Emily began to squirm, perhaps picking up on the radiating hatred that began to pour from Marilyn's body.

Forcing herself to stay under control, Tara calmly replied, "Well, as always, you would know, dear Aunt." Her smile was sickly and openly false. She would fight fire with fire and hope to not get burned. Marilyn strode back to the table and took a seat across from her.

"I do know. I care for my mother and look after my daughter. I laugh with my sister, and I look after the nieces *you've* chosen to neglect. Thank you for making such an excellent observation," Marilyn finished, knowing she had used her sharpest dagger in Tara's nieces. It was the one thing Tara had always regretted about leaving home. Those girls deserved to feel loved by their aunt — a feeling Tara had never known herself. She felt the heat rise in her face.

"Yes, you are quite the epitome of familial love. I know being berated and snipped at by you as a child brought me unequivocal joy and happiness. When you told me I was fat, when you told me I was stupid, that was you loving me and doing your family a favor, wasn't it?"

"I don't know what you're talking about. You were an awful child."

"I was a fine child. In fact, I was very astute and down-to-earth. Do you think I would keep you in my life, when all you've ever done is cut me down?"

"Honesty isn't a put-down, Tara. It's a way for you to grow."

"You want honesty, you goddamn lush?" Tara spat as she rose from her seat, unable to contain herself. Years of repression were flying out of her beyond her control. She was ready to strangle the woman if it meant the truth would squeeze from her mascara-caked eyes. She felt a steely hand on her shoulder and whipped around to see her father, his eyes like fire.

"Go outside, Tara."

"Defending her again, Dad? Want to know why I never came home?"

"I said, 'Go outside.'" His voice brooked no argument. Tara stared him down for what seemed like an eternity. Then, as always in the presence of her father, she caved. She stormed out of the kitchen without looking back, imagining the catlike grin her aunt no doubt displayed now that she was, yet again, ostracized for defending herself.

She stepped out into the mint-scented air that was slightly chilled with the remembrance of spring but warm enough to portend the arrival of summer. She stared at the pear tree. Her father, with whom she had never had a solid conversation, had always been her defender on some level. When she got in a car accident at sixteen with the new car he had bought for her, he gave her no criticism or grief. He simply fixed the car and moved forward. He paid for her college education and made no comment about the money she spent on food or beers out with friends. Whenever anything broke, he fixed it. Whenever she needed him, he came.

He always won when it came to family because it was the only thing he asked in return for saving her. He was the father, the provider, and he took that role seriously . . . but he was still enslaved by his family's idea of unity — the idea that a man could die, and a young girl could be solicited for sex by her uncle and tortured mercilessly by her aunts and nothing would be done. Because family is family.

Too angry to cry, Tara stormed over to the tree and sat down, leaning her head against the trunk. *I'll never make it*, she thought. If this was week one, how long would it take for her to break her father's heart by fighting back against her aunts? How would her mother fare with the conflict she could no longer avoid? She heard the door open and close softly.

"You're right, you know," Ali said. "She just doesn't want to be wrong."

Tara sighed. "I know. I just wish Dad would stand up for us for once."

"Oh, he is," Ali said, a smirk in her voice. Tara glanced at her, confused.

"Don't worry, I had Harold take the girls to the basement during your argument. You were too fired up to notice." *Harold is a decent sort of fellow,* Tara thought. At least he had the good sense to try and keep her nieces out of this mess. Then, Tara realized what Ali was saying.

"Dad's defending me in there?"

"Yeah," she breathed, clearly impressed. "I've never seen him so angry. Marilyn is actually cowering. . . . I should probably be in there taking video for you to watch, just so you know how much he really does love you."

"Yeah, sure," Tara said. She wished she could believe it. Love meant so much more than what he had provided. Love meant that he would have stood up for her a long, long time ago.

The two sisters sat in silence waiting for the storm to come outside and find them once again. As if on cue, the door opened and Tara heard voices. Unsure of whether they were angry or not, she remained rooted to the ground. Her mother's voice stood out first.

"Tara, we're leaving. Let's go, honey." Her tone was consoling, which was also new. So far, Tara had received kind words from her grandmother, a defense from her father, and consolation from her mother. Strange.

She made her way to the car. Her father joined them soon after, and they drove home in silence. No words were exchanged whatsoever for the rest of the night, and Tara found herself tucked into bed at nine thirty, staring up at the smoothly painted ceiling. She prayed for some guidance on how to survive her current predicament while doing the best she could to help her mother. Abject silence ensued.

Heaven didn't feel like answering just yet.

•••

Chapter Nine

Sometimes it was worth fighting sleep, if only to avoid the dreams.

•

It was another long weekend at Grandma Eve's. Their parents were on their annual Vegas vacation with their aunts and uncles. Tara and Ali did their best to stay united against Sam Jr., but they didn't last long before he had them turned on each other, tearing each other's hair out.

On the second day, Grandma Eve took them all fishing. Sam thought it would be funny to catch a crawdad and fling the pincered creature at Tara. It latched on to her skin for a brief moment before she flicked it off, resulting in a nasty cut. She winced and began to cry a little, and when Grandma Eve glanced over from the old picnic bench, she rolled her eyes and went right back to her magazine. Tara sat out the rest of the afternoon and watched Sam enjoy the rest of his time with Ali. She was so excited to be getting positive attention from him that she simply ignored Tara. Tara could still feel the sting on her wrist.

Once they were home, Grandma Eve headed to her bedroom for the night to watch TV. Grandpa Jon had recently cleaned the hot tub, and the girls had spent the first few nights enjoying the warm bubbles.

Tara decided to get into the warm water again that night and allow the events of the day to pass.

The three grandkids changed into their swimsuits and made their way over to the covered tub. The girls splashed around a little but mostly just did their best to try and look cool. Then, Sam came up with an idea for a game they had only vaguely heard about.

"It's called a hickey," he said. The girls were, and had always been, far too easy to manipulate. The worst was when they began to cry and he had to find a way to shut them up before getting in trouble . . . not that trouble was more than a scold and a dirty look. Being the only boy in the family did have its benefits.

"I've heard of those before," Ali chimed in, clearly proud that she knew what he was talking about. "It's the funny mark on your neck you get from making out."

Tara cringed. "That's gross."

"No, it's not; it's fun," Sam cajoled. He stared down the girls with a sly intensity in his teenage eyes. "Why don't you let me give you one?"

Tara and Ali looked at each other. On the one hand, they knew what he was saying was bad — they were children, and the thought of being sucked on by a teenager gave Tara the creeps. On the other hand, their elder cousin, who had control over what their grandparents allowed them to do at all times, wanted them to take on a dare.

"I'll do it," Ali said boldly. Tara saw that she was scared, but she didn't say anything. She was too scared to, as she always was when they were left alone with him.

Sam pulled Ali in close and sucked hard on her neck. She squirmed but tried to play off how awful it felt. When he was finished, he pushed her away and laughed.

He glanced at Tara. "You next!"

"No," Tara murmured. "I don't want to."

"Oh, come on, you big baby. It's not like it hurts. Does it, Ali?"

"Not really. . . . It's fine, Tara. Just do it."

Tara stared at them for a minute before Sam swam over and cornered her and sucked on her small neck. He bit with his teeth to get it really good. She closed her eyes and waited for it to be over. When he finally backed away, she sank into the water up to just below her nose to wash his spit off her neck.

They went to sleep in the usual way that night: Sam sprawled out on the floor, and Ali and Tara next to him, pressed as far away from him as possible as they breathed in the rancid stench of cat piss. The next morning, Gran and Grandma Eve came in to wake them up. The arrangement had been to split the babysitting in half so that Eve and Jon wouldn't get too overwhelmed with so many children around — children they weren't watching. When Gran saw the girls, she froze.

"What is this?" she asked, her voice cold as ice. Tara had never heard her sound like that.

"What?" Eve asked. Gran lifted a section of Tara's long brown hair, revealing the sexual mark to the room at large. She went over to Ali and discovered the same. Sam Jr., who had been standing beside them, was suddenly nowhere to be found.

Gran marched right up to Grandma Eve, and Tara thought she was going to spit in her face.

"You will never watch these children again, you neglectful bitch! I'm calling Social Services on you and that boy. You should be ashamed of yourself," she finished, her voice violent with rage. She herded the girls to the car, and as they buckled themselves in, Tara felt a stab of relief mingled with a pinch of joy. They would never being staying with Grandma Eve again!

Gran got into the driver's seat and turned back to look at her little girls. There were tears in her eyes.

"I won't ever let them hurt you again, okay girls? You let me know if something like this ever happens again. Understood?"

"Yes, Gran," they replied. The rest of the weekend passed fairly quickly, and then their parents returned home and were told what happened. Tara and Ali never knew what they did to punish Sam Jr. for what he did, and no mention of the incident was ever made again. But Gran was true to her word. They never spent another night at Grandma Eve's.

•

Tara awoke to the mouthwatering scent of bacon and toast. She stretched her limbs and glanced over at her alarm clock. Ten thirty . . . the latest she had slept in since God knows when. Of course, tossing and turning with fitful dreams meant she was not as rested. Before falling asleep the night before, she'd decided that it would be in everyone's best interest if she were to stay away from her aunts. But the promise of hot bacon was irresistible. She threw the covers aside and made her way downstairs to the kitchen. Claire was at the stove flipping the pieces onto a paper towel-covered plate.

"Sleep well?" she asked.

"As well as possible," Tara replied. She took a place at the kitchen table and stared out the window at the house next door.

"Do you want some tea? There's a hot pot on the stove."

"Sure," Tara replied. Last night's events were being conveniently ignored. This was one instance that actually helped Tara. Her mother scooped some eggs, bacon and toast on a plate, filled a mug with hot water, and delicately dipped a tea bag into it. Watching the translucent skin around her mother's hand as she did this, Tara rose and carried her own plate and mug to the table, unwilling to allow her frail mother to do it for her. No protest came from Claire.

They ate in comfortable silence for a few minutes before Claire made an announcement. "I'm going to the farmers market today for vegetables," she said. "I would like you to come with me."

Tara almost laughed at her serious tone. It was as though she were discussing some kind of road trip that a teenager would abhor, rather than a quick jaunt to the outdoor market on a sunny summer day.

"That sounds fun. When would you like to leave?"

"As soon as you get dressed and finish your breakfast," Claire said as she stood to carry her plate to the kitchen sink. Tara couldn't help but notice that she'd hardly touched her food, and her heart sank with worry. But what could she do?

She took the last few bites of her toast and rinsed the dishes before placing them in the dishwasher. Although she wasn't the cleanest person in the world, she would not add to her mother's burden if she could help it. The weather was extremely agreeable. It was looking to be a beautiful day. Tara ran upstairs and threw on a white summer dress with yellow flowers and sandals. She tied her hair back with a long white ribbon.

Claire was waiting for her downstairs with keys in hand.

"Wow, you really take vegetables seriously, don't you?" Tara joked. She was indulged with a playful smirk.

"I most certainly do," she replied as she opened the door and led the way. They pulled out of the driveway and made their way toward I-25.

"Where is this place?" Tara asked. Why were they going so far out of the way for vegetables?

"We're going to Boulder. The pickings up there are my favorite," Claire stated, changing lanes to avoid a speeder coming up fast from behind. Tara didn't question her logic and began staring out the windshield at the rolling hills on the left and the towering mountains to the right. This place really was beautiful; she was usually just too distracted to notice. The mountains in the distance were so idyllic as to resemble a painting, blankets of snow resting on their rugged peaks.

After exiting the highway, they made their way down winding roads until the towering buildings of the CU Boulder college campus came into view. As the semester had recently come to an end, there was a distinct lack of college students roaming the parks and fields. Here the mountains seemed even more majestic, soaring high above the little shops and parks. Tara observed the locals, who had what one might call a granola persona about them. These people preferred bikes to cars, organic to cheap, and dreadlocks to showers. It was a culture of its own.

They pulled into a lot next to a soccer field and stepped out into the fresh mountain air. Tara stretched and admired the view. There was something about Boulder that conveyed a stronger sense of humanity. The people smiled more. Nature was more apparent and less man-made. She really enjoyed it. The two fell in stride, and they made their way toward the market.

They passed by some bakers' tents and breathed in the enticing smells of little tarts and loaves of fresh bread. Several tents had perfectly good vegetables, yet her mother pressed on in her mission. Her strange approach to an endeavor so simple sure was entertaining. Suddenly, Claire stopped.

"Ah, here we are!" she exclaimed as she beelined for a particularly large tent with a variety of options. She began examining pieces of vegetation closely, as though she were searching for a cure for the common cold.

"Tara?"

She turned at the sound of her name and found herself face-to-face with Tom Sanders. Today he wore a bright-purple shirt with a logo on it: Sanders' Organic Farm. His khaki shorts and hiking boots clashed with the neon hue, but naturally, he didn't seem to notice. A patch of black stubble lined his round cheeks and the curve of his chin. Somehow he managed to look more rugged than Tara remembered from the airport. Had it really only been a week since they boarded that plane? Tara groaned inwardly and then realized that she was gaping at him in silence.

"Uh, hey, Tom! It didn't occur to me that we might run into you here," she said. She really was the most awkward person on the planet sometimes. Ugh. But Tom was not deterred from continuing the conversation, for which she was grateful.

He smiled. "I'm so glad to see that you haven't turned into a vampire. When you didn't reply to my last text, I figured they had declared your texting me treason and punished you severely for your insubordination."

A pang of guilt struck her belly. "Actually, that is exactly what happened. Finally, after I repented and made my vampire intentions known, I was released to retrieve foodstuffs for the slaves."

"Ah, that does make sense. I can't tell you how happy I am to see you alive, and in the sunlight even! My serum shall be packed away for another day, but if you need it, you let me know."

"I appreciate that, Tom Sanders. You are truly a hero to us all." She smiled broadly. To hear a friendly voice after so much anger and fighting was like getting a flood of water after a drought.

He beamed back at her. "Well, well, well. Look what we have here: a genuine smile from the most morose and depressed girl on the planet. This state must be treating you better than you think."

"I wouldn't go that far . . .," she said as she rolled her eyes.

"I believe I have yet to make you laugh properly, though. There's still progress to be made." That look of determination sprung up from deep behind his eyes.

"I wouldn't hold your breath," she smirked. Was she a project for him? A broken puzzle in need of fixing? Did it matter? She felt more relaxed in this moment than she had since touching down at DIA.

"Hi, Tommy!" Claire said as she came up behind Tara and put her hands on her shoulders. "I see you've met my Tara. Isn't she just lovely?"

"Mom . . .," Tara said with an adolescent groan. She didn't need to listen to her mother making sure Tom knew she was very, very single. Her face grew warm with embarrassment. She glanced up briefly to see Tom smile down warmly at her. This resulted in more blushing, which made it all worse — a vicious cycle.

"She is, Claire. As a matter of fact, we already know each other!" he said, winking at Claire. What was that about? Claire's hands tensed ever so slightly on her shoulders, but her reply was jovial.

"Do you now? Well, that is quite the coincidence. Why don't you two go over to the teahouse and relax while I do my shopping? Unless you need to man your tent, Tommy."

Tom glanced over at a few of his workers and told them that he would be taking a break. They smiled agreeably and told him to have at it. Tara saw the respect and adoration for Tom in their eyes and felt an odd mixture of pride and jealousy that she didn't like at all. Tom stepped outside the tent and waited for her to join him on a stroll.

"So, what is this teahouse?" Tara asked as she glanced around at the various wares being sold, mostly to keep herself from staring at Tom. He was a lot more attractive than she remembered; her insides were doing terribly wonderful twirly things.

"It's pretty neat, actually. See?"

Tara pried her gaze away from his and landed on what appeared to be a temple. The walkway was lined with rosebushes that led to an ornate opening decorated with puzzle-like designs. Metal tables visible just inside hosted a plethora of patrons drinking various types of exotic teas. There was a small river on the side of the temple swirling in a constant regenerative flow. Tom gestured toward the front door, and Tara gasped as she stepped inside and took in the surroundings.

It was as though she had stepped into another country, another world. The ceiling was painted in a vast rainbow of colors. Carvings lined the pillared walls. The room was lined with tables and statues, and a decorative plant structure stood in the middle. A young hostess with a polka-dot dress and matching headband led them to a small table and handed them both menus.

"Do you like it?" Tom asked, his perpetual smile in place.

"I do. This is amazing . . . Tommy," she joked. He laughed. What a coincidence her mother knew him. . . . What were the odds?

"Your mother's always called me that since we were introduced at the stand last summer. Didn't have the heart to tell her not to."

"That's very kind of you."

"Not particularly. There are much worse nicknames one can have."

"I suppose there are." Suddenly, he leaned in closer with an uncharacteristically serious expression. "Now tell me how you're really faring, Miss Tara Kingston of the Littleton Kingstons."

Tara stared him down. His eyes really were a disconcerting shade of blue. With his hair so dark and his skin slightly tan, they shone out like lighthouse beacons in a storm. She wanted to reach out and find a home in those depths, but her storm was not his affair, no matter how well he knew her mother. Luckily, the waiter came over to take their order. She ordered a drink involving some kind of peach tea and a glass of white wine. Tom ordered some exotic-sounding tea she'd never heard of.

"So, you come here often?" she asked.

"No-no. No changing the subject. Do you know how worried I've been? . . . I mean, not that I've thought of you often. It's just that when your mom didn't come last week, I figured something must be wrong," he said. She felt her cheeks flush again at his slip and the pressure of having to talk about her current situation.

"Something has always been wrong. Me coming here hasn't changed that. It's all glossed over as usual, except . . ." Except for last night, when she called her aunt a goddamn lush and stormed out of her grandmother's house. She didn't want Tom Sanders to know that she had that side to her. She had just figured it out herself.

"Maybe what you need is to get away," he said as he stared at her attentively.

"I did get away. As you may remember, I am here very much against my own will."

He smoothed his fingers along the white linen tablecloth. His expression was closed. Had she upset him?

"I remember, Tara. I meant get away while you're here. The arrangement was that you'd stay in Colorado, right? You don't have to stay exactly where they are."

She stared at him. Was he seriously asking what she thought he was asking?

"I'm not sure what you're getting at, Tom Sanders," she said. If he was ignorant enough to think that she would just hop on up to Boulder with him, a near stranger, then he was out of his handsome little mind.

"Have you ever heard of the WWOOF program?" he asked.

"Woof program? What is that, like a shelter for lost dogs or something?"

He smiled at that, his usual joviality returning. "No, not 'woof.' W-W-O-O-F. It stands for Worldwide Opportunities on Organic Farms. It's a sort of exchange program where you agree to work on a farm and in return learn how to become self-sustaining. You work for room and board and use it as a learning experience, while the farmer gets the help he needs."

"You want me to work on your farm?"

"Well, why not? I already know you, so that helps weed out the possibility of you being a crazy person. We really could use some help this summer, and you could use something to keep your mind off of being in such a hated place," he said, the last bit with just an ounce of sarcasm. Did he resent her for hating his home? Most Coloradans she knew did, after all, but she had hoped that Tom would understand. Clearly, he didn't.

"And you think my mother is going to go for that? It's taken her years to even try to guilt me back — "

"Yes." Clearly, he was determined to convince her of his case. "And wouldn't she be thrilled to have you out of the house, not too far away, and happier?"

He does have a point — almost too close of a point, she thought. How much had Claire told him exactly?

Their drinks arrived, and Tara stared at Tom's crystal goblet of tea. The water was almost completely translucent, and sitting at the bottom was a ball of leaves. It looked strange and unnatural. Tara's peach tea wine, however, was exactly what she needed, and she took a replenishing sip from her tall-stemmed glass.

"What is that?" she asked, staring at the ball of twine in his cup.

"It's tea," he replied matter-of-factly.

"It's water with a lump of trees in it," she replied.

"You'll see. This is a lesson in things not always being what they seem." He winked. Suddenly, Claire appeared in the doorway. When her eyes found Tara's, she made her way over to their table.

"Excellent produce as always, Tommy," she said as she pulled up a chair and set her bags on the floor.

"Thank you, ma'am," he said, tipping an invisible cowboy hat. "Actually, I was just proposing that your daughter become something of a farmer herself."

"Oh?" she replied, glancing curiously from Tara to Tom and back. He explained the WWOOF program, and how Tara would have her own apartment space and could maybe, possibly be happier there. Claire was ecstatic, and Tara knew instantly that any case she would make would be lost.

"Well, Tara, I think if Tommy needs your help . . .," she said breezily.

"Seriously? After all you did to get me here?" That turned her mother's expression upside down.

"Tara, we can't keep having incidents like last night. I'm grateful that you came out, even if it is only out of guilt, but I think it's best we keep you at a short distance for a while."

Tara ignored the barb. "So now you want to get rid of me? What, did Marilyn suggest it and this convenient situation just happened to arise today?"

"No! For heaven's sake, don't be so suspicious, Tara. I'm thinking of you here. It is very clear that you hate it back home. We're only a half-hour away." She glanced at Tom and asked, "Would we be allowed to visit her?"

"Of course," he replied. "Anytime you'd like! We love having large dinners at the farm."

"Suddenly I feel as though the decision has already been made for me," Tara mumbled. Tom looked crushed by her statement.

"Oh, Tara, please don't think that! Of course the choice is yours. I just wanted to provide an opportunity for this to maybe be a little easier for you. This way, you'll only see who you want and avoid the ones you don't," he finished delicately. He was succeeding at pretending that her mother wasn't airing out their problems to him. Tara glanced from Tom to her mother. It wouldn't be the worst thing in the world to retreat from her aunts, to go where her parents and sister and nieces could come and spend time together without the tension.

She took another sip of her wine. "Well, how soon can I move in?"

•••

Chapter Ten

Tara stared out her bedroom window, her gaze seeing far past the Rocky Mountains. One of the distant towering peaks reminded her of a roller coaster she'd once ridden long ago. She sighed as her mind drifted easily into the memory.

Tara was five years old. It was her first trip to Orlando, and she beamed as she gazed around at the decorative hotels and palm trees. Her dad had rented a red convertible just like she wanted, and the humid Florida air tossed her hair around like Medusa's serpents. In spite of the strands whipping her face, Tara had never been happier.

She looked over at Ali, who was admiring the foreign scenery with pure delight. She caught her sister's eye and they high-fived, ecstatic about new adventures. They checked in at the Walt Disney World Dolphin Hotel, which was an attraction in itself. Ali insisted on opening the hotel room door with her very own key, and they burst inside and ran straight to a small veranda overlooking a long boardwalk filled with carnival-style games.

She turned to face their parents, her eyes pleading, and said, "Can we please do the boardwalk games first? Please?"

Tara's father lifted a skeptical eyebrow. "We're steps away from Walt Disney World and you want to go play ring toss?"

Much as he tried to reason with them, the girls refused to be moved. They walked along the hotel's long boardwalk winning game after game, their arms becoming full with irrationally large stuffed animals. When they could carry no more, they opted to drop everything back at the room before boarding a boat headed toward the Magic Kingdom.

Once in the park, Claire sat patiently with their belongings as Bob took the girls on every ride whose height requirement they met, from Space Mountain to Splash Mountain. They walked up Main Street to the famous Disney Castle, a real-life version of the magical one Tara had seen at the beginning of every Disney movie. To sum it up: Tara was in five-year-old heaven.

One day, as she was making her way down a crowded main street, she saw a hat with ears on it in a nearby store. Excited, she walked straight over and into the shop, leaving her family behind.

She picked up the hat, put it on, and admired in a shop mirror how it looked on her little head. She walked around, gazing in awe at the rows and rows of candy, clothing, and toys that seemed to have no end. After a while she turned in a circle to realize that no one had followed her there — she was alone. She paced around the store and then finally stepped back out onto the street.

"Tara!" her mother called, both relief and annoyance tingeing her voice. An employee came out of the store, presumably to retrieve the hat that hadn't been paid for. Claire grabbed it from Tara's head and handed it roughly to the young sales girl, who turned around immediately to head back into the store so as to not be a part of the scene. Claire knelt down on her knees and held Tara firmly by the arms.

"Don't you ever walk away like that again, Tara. Do you hear me?" she said.

Tears began to fall down Tara's face, and she nodded emphatically. The experience was overwhelming — the fear of being lost and feeling bad that she had upset her mother. Tara hated being in trouble.

Claire swept her up into a fierce hug and whispered in her ear, "Don't you see, Tara? If I can't see you, how can I protect you and keep you safe?" Of course she understood; no one could look after her like her mother could, after all. She would try to remember not to walk too far away again.

Tara stared with glazed-over eyes at her repacked suitcase, amazed at the events of the past week. What had started out as a dreaded trip to the homeland had suddenly become a farmland adventure, and her heart was beating a little faster. Since leaving Colorado, she had become a city person. She was a Bostonian. She ate lobster and drank Sam Adams Oktoberfest beer in the radiant autumn months. The fact that she was willing to try on rustic farm life was a pretty sure indicator of how dedicated she was to reinventing herself . . . or how dedicated she was to running away. In that moment, it was tough to tell which one won out.

Tara hefted her bags back down the carpeted staircase to the garage door and then made her way toward the kitchen. At any given time, Claire was likely to be found in one of two places: the kitchen or the garden. At the moment, she was in the kitchen packing a small picnic lunch.

"Hey," Tara said, announcing her presence. That was another thing: Claire was a rather oblivious woman. She was also very serious about proper nutrition and took great care in putting meals together. The picnic included several varieties of fruits and vegetables, as well as a turkey and cheese sandwich with no mayo.

"Hey," Claire replied, glancing up. "Are you still a fan of turkey and cheese?"

"I am."

"Good. Let me just finish putting this together, and then we can head on up."

"Do you really think this is the right solution, Mom?"

Claire paused before shoving the sandwich into a plastic baggie. She looked up and gazed into her daughter's eyes. "I do think that you're miserable here. I think I spent all that effort to get you to come home and now I almost regret doing it. You've grown shadows under your eyes, and behind those shadows all I can see is anger. I don't like seeing that in you, Tara."

"Don't you think it's warranted?"

"Of course it is. I've seen how they've been with you since you returned. And for the first time, your father finally let himself see it, too. You know they'll never bother to come see you out there, and without transportation, you have a perfect excuse not to come back here. I see no better solution, nor would I have faith in anyone but Tommy to bring some joy back into your life," she finished with a sly grin. Tara ignored it.

"What happens if something happens to you?" Tara asked. She was afraid to, but she couldn't resist. Claire's expression shuttered, effectively hiding her emotions, and Tara almost regretted bringing it up. Still, she needed to know. Despite everything, Claire was the primary reason she was here. If that meant enduring the wrath of her snotty aunts, then so be it.

"If I get worse, we will send someone out to get you so we can be together in the final days," she said, her tone matter-of-fact.

"How can you talk about it like that? Like it's just another errand to run?"

Claire smiled sadly, her wrinkled face appearing significantly more aged than her fifty years. When had those wrinkles appeared?

"Death is a part of life, Tara. Everyone knows that. We can either live in fear and receive none of what it has to bring, or we can accept and embrace it. I'd rather spend this time watching my children be happy. In your case, that means placing you away from the family . . . just not so far that I can't come see you at least once a week."

Claire finished wrapping up Tara's lunch and placed it all in a brown paper bag, rolling the top down as far as it would go. Her silence indicated an end to the discussion, and Tara slowly rose and brought her belongings out to the car. She thought about the weeks ahead and what she would do if her mother's condition worsened. Deep down she knew it wasn't a matter of *if* but *when*.

Shaking her head, she removed all thoughts of it and buckled her seat belt, focusing instead on the present moment.

Tom Sanders waved from the bright-purple farmhouse at the end of the long dirt road, having recognized Claire's car. In spite of himself, he had to admit that he was nervous.

When Claire told him of her terminal illness and her daughter's unwillingness to come home, his heart nearly broke. She had become a dear friend of his over the years; she was a very loyal customer. They had often spent much time talking, and as a result, Tom knew more about Tara than he was willing to admit to her . . . at least for a while. When Claire gave him a copy of the flight itinerary, he stared at her in bemusement. She couldn't be serious . . .

It was true that Tom did have a way with people, and his view of life had an ability to help many in their darkest hours. He had given several inspirational speeches throughout college and his twenties, and although he had been offered several jobs in Denver and beyond, he couldn't consider leaving the family farm. Not that they needed him — it was quite the other way around. He had been lucky enough to find his happiness at a young age, with his hands in the dirt and sweat on his brow. The joy he had felt growing up on a farm was something he had always wanted to share, and because of this he had spent most of his time helping others find the same.

And now he had Tara Kingston on his hands. Part of him felt guilty about deceiving her like this. He knew the minute he saw her in that airport who she was, but he didn't expect to find her so witty and charming. You would think that someone who had as positive an outlook as Tom would find love easily, but he never had. For some reason, no one ever seemed right.

He had never felt that strange twisting in his gut, that lightness of step that he felt after his first exchange with Tara. He had been selfish in getting her here, and he knew it. But if this were a solution for her, wouldn't the ends justify the means? After all, he could never deny a dying woman's last wish.

Claire's little green compact car rolled up and parked in the dirt lot in front of the main farmhouse. He took a deep, steadying breath before making his way down the wooden porch steps to meet them. Tara was gazing around with wonder and trepidation in her eyes. Perhaps she wasn't a country girl; she might be later. They stepped out of the car, and Claire greeted him warmly.

"Tommy! It's so good to see you," she crooned as she gave him a surprisingly tight hug. "I think you're just the ticket," she whispered into his ear. He tried to smile back, but it came out as a shy smirk instead.

"You, too. Hi, Tara. Ready to become a farmer?" he asked playfully. If it was the last thing he did, he would chase the darkness from Tara Kingston's eyes and replace it with glowing, exuberant light. Not that they needed much; the dark-blue color nearly matched his own. . . . You know, if you were to observe those kinds of things.

"I certainly hope so," she replied before reaching into the car to pull out her bags.

"Oh, please. Allow me," Tom said. He hurried over and reached for her black tote and matching suitcase. Their hands brushed, and he froze. He struggled to find something witty to say — anything at all, really — and for the first time in his life came up empty. Seconds passed before Tara's curious stare woke him from his small reverie, though to Tom they felt like minutes.

"Just guessing the contents of these bags. You know, for storage reasons," he said, winking at her. *Nice save,* he thought.

"Uh-huh," Tara replied. "Thanks."

He took the bags from her and led the way to the house.

"Your apartment is just up here," he said while stepping inside. The farmhouse, with its bright-purple hue, was something entirely unique. They grew various herbs in the greenhouse out back, stored milk and cheese in the massive freezer in the basement, and enjoyed meals together with the fruits of their labor in the warm country kitchen that was the center of the home. A staircase led to a small apartment that they had built specifically for visiting farmhands, and it had seen many over the years. Because Coloradans were so conscious of supporting their local farms, the Sanders clan had prospered over the years, though they had not lived extravagantly. Tom's mother had instilled in him a value of simplicity, which Tom found brought a sense of inner peace not often found in the greatest of mansions.

Tom carried Tara's bags up the narrow staircase, and she followed right behind.

"Where are the other rooms?" she asked.

"There's another staircase just on the other side of the kitchen. All the other rooms are up there. And the laundry is just off the kitchen. You'll get a proper tour, don't worry."

"Ah," she said as they reached the top of the stairs. They walked through the wooden door to her bedroom. The walls were painted a light sage color, the borders a fresh shade of cream. The queen-sized farmhouse bed had a multicolored patchwork quilt turned down at the top to reveal white cotton sheets and two fluffy pillows. The walls sported various paintings of Colorado wildflowers, showcasing the contrast of colorful flora and fauna with dark, imposing mountains.

"Well! Isn't this something?" Claire exclaimed in admiration.

Tom chuckled. "My mother is a painter, and she took a lot of pride in putting this room together. If there's one thing she's good at, it's making a space feel like home."

Tara glanced at him before gazing down at the floor. Tom wondered what was on her mind but stayed silent.

"Well, I think this will do very nicely," Claire announced as she made her way toward the door.

Picking up on the social cue, Tom said, "Would you like something to eat or drink before you go, Claire? We have plenty of fresh produce . . . enough to pull off a decent lunch, anyway."

"No, thank you, Tommy. I've got a family dinner to get to in a few hours," she said, making her way down the stairs. Tom paused in the doorway as Tara continued to stare at the ground as though she were attempting to suppress tears. He walked over to her and put his hand gently on hers, which startled her into jumping a foot away from him.

"Whoa there, Nelly. I'm not gonna hurt ya," he said, trying to lighten the mood.

"Sorry," she said, quickly moving out of reach toward the door. Tom tried to suppress the hurt he felt at her refusal to be touched by him, even consolingly. It was clear that whatever walls she had put up were solid . . . perhaps even unbreakable. No one would be able to tear them down but her, but that didn't stop him from wanting to help the process along. He followed her down the stairs and back out to the porch, where Claire stood patiently waiting for them. In a surprising move, Tara rushed to her mother and wrapped her in her arms, hugging her as tight as she could.

"You'll come to visit soon, right?" she asked, as though she were a child being left at summer camp. Suddenly the thought of not having a car and being away from her mother, with whom she had just rekindled a delicate relationship, was borderline terrifying. What would she do in this place half-foreign, half-home?

Claire held her tightly and whispered, "Of course we will, baby. I'll bring your sister and nieces, too. I'm sure Maddie would go nuts with so much to explore."

"You're welcome anytime, Claire," Tom said gallantly.

Claire pulled Tara away and held her at arm's length, as if to examine her readiness. "You take care of her, Tommy," she said, her eyes still on Tara. "Lord knows you might be the only one able to do it."

"Hey now . . .," Tara said.

"She'll get a nice dog bowl and a cup of water, just like everyone else," Tom joked from behind her. She remembered how amusing he had been at the airport and suddenly felt heartened by this plan.

"There. See? Just what you need," Claire said, stroking her cheek lovingly before turning down the wooden steps. She blew a kiss out the car window and drove down the dirt road. Tara felt a strong sense of relief watching her go, knowing that she wouldn't have to be at family dinner tonight, that she might finally be able to relax. She turned back toward Tom and found him watching her cautiously.

"I'm not going to break, you know," she said.

"I know that. . . . I just worry sometimes."

"You? Tom Sanders, Mr. Sunshine and Daisies? I have a difficult time believing that, sir." Tara had forgotten how fun it was to flirt.

"You are very mistaken, madam. In fact, I prefer to go by Mr. Unicorns and Butterflies, but you're new, so I'll allow the mistake . . . this time."

"Ah, well I thank you gratuitously for your consideration. You've no idea what it means to be living with so lenient a master."

"I do try. Now, what say you get comfortable and settle in, and afterwards I'll give you a tour of the place?"

"That sounds lovely. You can show me where my cup of water and dog bowl will be stationed."

"Yes, I imagine somewhere near the pigpen would be appropriate."

"You have a pigpen?"

"Well, no, but if you'd like one to be near your food, I'm sure we could make arrangements. We're very accommodating here at the Sanders Farm."

"How reassuring," she mumbled. "I'm heading to my room now."

"Meet back in the kitchen in an hour or so?"

"Sounds good," she replied, making her way up to her new country quarters. She closed the door gently behind her and leaned her back against it, surveying the room. A month ago, if anyone had asked where Tara Kingston would soon be headed, "some stranger's farm in Boulder, Colorado," would not have been remotely close to her first answer. Yet here she was. She approached her suitcase yet again. Packing and unpacking had become an acquired skill while moving around in college, though it was not something she particularly loved to do.

Upon opening the closet, she found a wealth of empty hangers. Across from the bed was a small, dark wooden dresser with three wide drawers. The room really was homey. She unpacked her things and explored this new space, reminding herself to avoid three specific thoughts: her mother's illness, her family's drama, and, of course, Tom Sanders' perfectly shaped, kissable mouth.

•••

Chapter Eleven

Tom sat with a laptop at the kitchen table, evaluating the online Farmer's Almanac for any new tips or data he might need. As he meandered his way through various articles, his ears perked up at the sound of approaching footsteps coming from the far staircase. He looked up as Tara made her way into the room. She was wearing a simple pair of dark jeans with trendy boots and a plain black T-shirt. Her hair was pulled back in a ponytail, showing her eyes off to great advantage. She smiled warmly as she took her seat at the long brown table.

"I like this kitchen," she said. "It's nice and big. This table is pretty big for a kitchen table, too."

"We get a lot of visitors, especially when we hire on more workers to help in the summer and fall months. Believe me, you'll think it feels small when we get the whole brood in here for dinner."

"Where is everyone, anyway?" It had been curiously quiet at the house since she arrived. She'd assumed that the place would be bustling with people. Tom shrugged.

"Planting, selling . . . doing various chores that need to get done. You'll meet some folks on our tour, I imagine. And then again at lunch. Everyone loves lunchtime. It's a hoot."

Tara settled against the back of her chair and took in the room. The cabinets were comprised of dark wood, but Tom's mother, the painter, had taken care to add various shades of red and blue paint for a splash of color. There was a large island in the center that sported a massive stovetop, like one on a cooking show. Counter space abounded, though much of it was covered with herbs and spices, and tins of flour and sugar and salt. Copper pots and pans hung from the ceiling, waiting to be used. A stainless steel fridge and oven set dominated the back wall. The floor was wooden as well, perhaps even the original wood. The room smelled of dried herbs and aged wood, which was not at all an unpleasant combination.

Tara glanced back at Tom, who looked completely at peace in his home. *It must be an amazing feeling,* she thought, *to be at home and have it feel like home.* He sported his usual khaki shorts and hiking boots, but he'd changed into a dark-blue T-shirt that brought out the color of his eyes, which crinkled at the corners as he smiled at her admiration of his hearth.

"Not too bad, eh?" he asked.

"I'll let you know after a day of work. You do realize, after all, that I am choosing slave labor over a comfortable yet nasty home a mere half-hour away," she replied. She felt a small sense of dread in the ignorance of what lay ahead for her daily life.

"Ha! I think you'll find the slave labor to be quite amenable to your needs, Tara Kingston. I'll open your eyes to the wonders of farm life."

He rose from the table, and she followed his lead out one of the back doors. This side of the house sported rows and rows of bare dirt prepped for planting. A massive white fence blocked in soil that would presumably house vegetables and fruits of some kind in the coming months. There were two smaller houses, one surrounded by a slew of white and black chickens, the other much larger, perhaps containing more animals. Tara imagined herself collecting eggs in the wispy light of dawn and felt a little tingle of excitement at trying something new. They made their way to the earthen rows of crops.

"This is where we'll be planting some potatoes, carrots, lettuce, and snow peas," he said, indicating various piles of dirt. "The garden over there will house broccoli, cucumbers, and pumpkins . . . probably a healthy number of tomatoes, too."

"Do you plant fruit as well?"

"We do," he replied. "We'll be having a strawberry festival in July, and the apple orchard should be bearing some good fruit come September. And there are some raspberry bushes out by the orchard that do pretty well."

"Sounds like a good feast," Tara said as she gazed around in awe.

Tom nodded, clearly very proud of his work.

"It is. It helps that so many people rely on what we can grow, and according to the almanac, it should be an excellent crop this summer. Ah, we've found a person!"

A woman in a broad-rimmed hat, weathered jeans rolled up to the calf, and a tattered, baggy T-shirt with a picture of a kitten was making her way over. Tara had to stifle a giggle at the ridiculous outfit, as the woman could very well be Tom's mother. Beneath her hat was shiny gray hair tucked into a short ponytail. Her eyes were warm and welcoming, and she approached Tara with open arms. Not knowing what else to do, Tara spread her arms to accept her for fear of causing insult.

"Ah, this must be our new farmhand!" she said, grasping Tara's forearms and giving her a thorough once-over. Her voice was like warm honey. Her blue eyes were sharp and intelligent.

"This is her," Tom beamed, stepping back to let the woman make her inspection. Tara almost gasped when she began to squeeze her forearms as though testing how tender she might be as a piece of meat.

"Good, strong arms. That's good. . . . You'll do well here. We are up at four in the morning every day and fall asleep at precisely five o'clock, right after dinner."

Tara stared. Seriously? Calling her mother to come pick her up began to sound like an excellent idea, but as Tara continued to stare, the woman's face crinkled and she laughed heartily.

"Oh, my poor child, you should have seen your face! I'm sorry. I'm sure you must not be used to joking around based on where you're coming from. I am Penny Sanders, Tom's mother and the head honcho of this establishment."

Tara wasn't sure how to respond to being the butt of her joke. What did she mean by her being unable to take one, anyway? How would she know?

"Yeah, you got me real good, Mrs. Sanders."

Penny threw her hands in the air in a dramatic gesture. "Oh, please call me Penny. I don't know what I'd do if you said 'Mrs. Sanders.' Far too stilted for my taste."

"I'm sorry. It's just what I learned to be respectful."

"I don't know many people or children around here who refer to their elders as Mr. or Mrs. So-and-So. Where did you pick up such manners?"

"New England," Tara replied, trying to keep the defensiveness out of her voice.

"Oh, New England is a wonderful place! I know Tommy loves going there and conversing with the other farmers. Good for you, good for you . . . Tara, is it?"

"Yes," Tara replied, appeased at her compliment. To hear trash-talking about her home of choice from strangers in her new sanctuary would be too much. However, Penny seemed absolutely oblivious to any discomfort she might be causing. She looped her arm inside Tara's and began leading them toward the orchard.

"You are most welcome here, Tara, and we're glad to have you. I think you'll find what we do here to be very rewarding, especially when the crops come into bloom and the fruits of your labor burst from the earth before your eyes. We usually have breakfast around eight and finish up the day at six, with a nice long lunch that may or may not include nap time for *some* people," she said as she glanced sideways at Tom, who shrugged.

"An hour-long nap is just the ticket to having a great rest of the day," he explained, winking at Tara. She began to get the impression that she had somehow wound up in the Land of Oz, where everyone smiled as they pranced arm in arm on a merry adventure. She wasn't sure what to think about it.

Penny and Tom led her through each part of the farm for the rest of the morning, introducing her to the chickens and goats, and showing her what would be planted where. It was a large stretch of land, and Tara found herself amazed every time she looked up to see towering blue mountains surrounding this little haven. Despite having grown up in their shadow, something about their presence made her feel safe. It was a foreign experience to a familiar sight. Once the official tour was over, Penny announced that she would show Tara how to cook up a country lunch, and they headed back to the house.

"Tom, you go on and help Ned with some planting. It looks like he's been falling behind a little this morning, which I'm certain has *nothing* to do with the rum and Coke party he enjoyed last night after dinner," she said. Tom gave them both a small salute and turned back toward the fields, where Tara had met a few of the other summer workers just before.

Penny stepped into the kitchen and reached into a drawer to pull out two aprons with colorful prints, both clearly homemade.

"Here you are," she said in a singsong voice as she handed Tara an apron with a green leaf pattern to tie around her waist.

"Are we going to be getting particularly dirty?"

Penny cast her a sideways glance. "No, but I like making aprons, and someone needs to wear them. If not us, then who?"

Tara chuckled at that and tied it firmly around her middle. "No one, I guess. You could always sell them," she offered. They were clearly very well-made.

"Oh, I do. Believe me, we have a lot of free time in the winter months. Makes for a substantial amount of sewing projects to sell in the spring."

"I see." The concept of being bored was interesting. After all, Boston never ran out of entertainment, even in the harsh winter months. Did country people really just sit around and stitch through them? How awful that must be.

Penny took down a large pot from the hanger and handed it to Tara. "Fill that with water, will you?" she asked. Tara obeyed and stood at the sink for several minutes before the massive pot was filled to an appropriate level. She then turned off the silver faucet and lugged the pot over to the stove.

"Go ahead and turn it up to high," Penny directed. She was chopping up fresh herbs from the greenhouse, which caused an earthy aroma to fill the room. Tara was intrigued to see what special dish she would make for the household. She watched Penny walk over to a cabinet and pull out a few boxes of whole-wheat pasta.

"A proper country lunch, huh?" Tara joked. She smirked as Penny checked the water for boiling and then set the boxes down in preparation.

"Now, now," she said. "Pasta has lots of carbs to keep everyone full of energy. Besides, you try feeding a houseful of people with enormous appetites. Spaghetti is a fan favorite simply because it doesn't take all day to put it together, and because I say so."

"I guess that makes perfect sense," Tara said, glancing down at her apron, which was now very obviously unnecessary — pasta wasn't exactly the messiest meal to make.

"It sure does. Also, come smell this herb combo I whipped up to add some flavor. I think you'll be pleased."

Tara walked over, though she really didn't need to. The sharp scent of basil and oregano had been floating in the air since Penny began chopping away.

"We keep it nice and fresh. It makes such a difference," Penny commented. The water was now boiling, so she broke the pasta in half and dropped it in. She then took a homemade can of . . . something . . . from the cupboard and began to open it with a can opener. Tara was surprised to see tomato sauce, bright and red.

"Did you make that?" she asked. She had never seen anything canned that didn't have a label and a clear expiration date.

"Yep! We'll teach you the technique once we get a good pile of tomatoes. It's great for fresh sauce in a pinch." After dumping a few cans into another pot and turning on the heat, she poured the chopped herbs into the mixture, as well as a few cloves of minced garlic and a bit of salt and pepper. She then made her way over to the refrigerator and pulled out a colorful jug.

"Fresh tea?" she asked Tara, who accepted a glass gratefully. She took a seat at the kitchen table with Penny. The bitter taste of the tea with a soft touch of sugar soothed her parched throat while replenishing her energy.

"So, tell me about yourself, Tara," Penny said, taking a sip of tea and eyeing her with the blue eyes she shared with her son. Tara leaned in.

"Well, you tell me what you already know, and I'll work on starting my story from there," Tara said, her eyes narrowed slightly. *'Based on where you're from.'* . . . It was clear that Penny already knew something about her. Penny leaned back in her chair, clearly undaunted.

"Well, I know everything that Tom knows. You should know that he and I have very few secrets, if any. I know why you're here. I know how you've been treated. And, most importantly, I think I know how to fix it."

"You think it's something that can be fixed?" Tara asked, a mixture of hope and disbelief battling for possession of her heart.

"I do," Penny confirmed. "There is not much that the earth cannot heal. I've learned this over the years, through the death of my husband especially. I learned to heal here, and I think you will, too."

"I'm sorry . . ." She was never sure how to respond to stories of death. Penny waved her hand again.

"It's all right, Tara. Death is a part of life. . . . It just so happened that I wasn't taken first. Could have happened to anyone, really. He's in a better place now."

"Right, yes," Tara said, thinking of her mother. How much time did she have left? Why did everyone keep talking about how natural death was? It wasn't natural to be taken by cancer before you were meant to go. It just wasn't. Tara looked down and saw Penny's hand covering her own. She looked up with watery eyes.

"You'll make it through, Tara," Penny said firmly. "You've got people that care about you now. You don't have to suffer alone."

"You met me like two hours ago."

Penny squeezed her hand firmly before releasing it and leaning back against her chair. "And in all that time, I've already learned to care for your well-being. Of course, it helps that Tom speaks so highly of you. I've never seen him go all meek and mild for a young lady," she said with a knowing smile. Tara felt herself blushing.

"Yes, well. Tom has been very kind to me. I'll remember his friendship fondly when I go back home." These people needed to know not to get too attached. Her time here would be temporary, and she couldn't risk hurting everyone in the situation by letting them believe that she would somehow see the light and decide to stay. It wasn't happening.

Penny's face fell slightly before she turned her motherly support mode back on. "Well, you do what's best for you, and we'll do our best to help you with whatever you need."

"I appreciate it," Tara said. To her relief, Penny dropped the subject and went back to the stove, where the pasta had finished cooking. Tara offered to set the table and was handed several maroon-colored plates and silver forks to disperse along the long wooden surface. As she was finishing, she saw Tom slide open the kitchen door and stroll in, his forehead beaded with sweat. He had a splash of dirt along his cheek, likely from the back of his right hand, which was dusted with flecks of earth.

"What's for lunch, womenfolk?" he asked.

"Nothing for you until those hands are clean. Also, to teach you gender equality, you will be in charge of dinner, Sonny Boy," Penny said.

"Uh-huh. Like that wasn't going to be the case anyway," he said with an eye roll and then looked at Tara. "We switch off who cooks meals so it doesn't become overwhelming. You'll be getting a nice dinner tonight, with my special skills!"

"Nothing beats my pasta," Penny said.

Tom made his way to the bathroom to wash up, followed by three others, a young woman and two men. A man who looked particularly green and slumped over took up the rear. He was obviously Ned. Tara felt sorry for him.

Penny dumped the sauce in with the pasta and stirred it up before lugging it over to the kitchen table, where the household was slowly gathering.

Tara took a seat and glanced up as Tom sat across from her. His hair was damp and spiked from a quick rinse in the sink. He looked boyish and playful, and Tara reminded herself once again what the consequences of getting too close to him would be. She didn't need to add heartbreak to her long list of Colorado issues. The removal of her gaze in no way deterred him from attempting to hold her attention.

"I'm excited to see that my mother didn't kill you with hard labor yet," he said, evoking a small laugh from her.

"I'm excited to see that you washed like a normal person," Penny chimed in as she took a seat. Looking at Tara, she added, "He usually never cleans himself so thoroughly, so, thank you, for that."

Tom turned a deep shade of red, and for the first time, Tara saw that he was capable of being embarrassed.

"So that makes you blush, but skipping gleefully through a crowded airport has no effect?" Tara asked, laughing along with his mother.

"I just felt like being cleaner today, that's all," he said with a bashful tone. He scooped a pile of spaghetti onto his plate and stared at it intently. This new shy Tom was like a stranger, and Tara wasn't particularly thrilled about it. She liked him when he was outgoing with clever retorts . . . not that she liked him at all.

Once the rest of the crew joined them at the table, Tara was introduced to everyone. Michael was an Irishman who had traveled abroad to get a taste of American culture. He was short with a weak chin, auburn hair, and a melodious accent. Tara felt as though she could listen to him all day and pretend to be on the Emerald Isle, a place she had always wanted to go. Curiously, Michael did not particularly like being Irish, and he longed to find a way to stay in America and celebrate a wild American St. Patrick's Day. According to him, that was a common view.

"St. Patrick's in Ireland can be wild, I grant yeh," he explained, "but it's more of a family affair. After all, 'tis a religious connotation, rather than a bunch of Americans clingin' to some form o' ethnicity. It's amazin' what people here do to try and prove they're Irish. . . . An', of course, the Irish think they're ridiculous."

"At least you aren't famous for living in igloos and having a moose for a pet," Kaily said. She was from Toronto, a bustling city with plenty of culture. However, every time she came to America, people believed that she lived in a remote ice castle and lived off maple syrup.

"I can't tell you how much I get teased when I say 'aboot' correctly," she finished. Tara stifled a giggle and exchanged a glance with Tom, who was doing the same. All of them had come for the WWOOF program except for Ned, who was born and raised in Boulder and a longtime friend of the family. He had turned twenty-one the month before, which explained his excitement at drinking when he saw fit — though the consequences were extremely apparent. He picked at his food and said little.

Kaily was twenty-two years old and just out of what she would call "university." Wanting to see a bit of the world first, she'd decided to get firsthand experience in sustainable farming in America, as her specialty had been agricultural preservation. She was well-informed on all things farming and had much to say on techniques that Tara could in no way understand. The natural elements in the earth and manure that were most conducive to a successful crop were discussed in some detail.

"When I emulated the test, we compared the results between organic fertilizer and a common chemical fertilizer to determine whether there really was a benefit to one over the other. Can you guess the results?"

Tara blinked and glanced over at Tom. His cheek dimpled as he cast her a sideways glance.

"I would guess that the organic compound was more successful, but I also read the same study," he said.

Kaily broke off a piece of her roll and tossed it at him from across the table. He laughed, popped the morsel into his mouth, and glanced at Tara.

Kaily continued, "Soil contains a lot of nutrients and chemicals that help the plants thrive, including pH balance. Organic manure has been proven time and time again to be more successful at producing exceptional crops. There is actually a great amount of science that goes into farming."

"So I hear," Tara said. She made a mental note to do some reading that night to improve her knowledge. Among this group, it was clear she was deeply uninformed, though they didn't make her feel inferior.

At the end of the meal, Ned had his head on the table, looking as though death would be a welcome reprieve. Penny looked at him sternly.

"All right, Ned, get your ass upstairs to bed, and let this be a lesson to you. No binge drinking before a workday!"

"Every day is a workday," Ned mumbled into the table.

Penny looked at Michael and said, "Michael, be a dear and carry this sorry excuse for a recent adult to his bedroom, would you?"

"Sure ting, Penny-mine," Michael said. Despite his short height, Michael was stocky, and he easily hefted the skinny young man over his shoulder and carried him to his room.

"Uhhh. I'm never drinking again," they heard Ned moan from down the hall, and they all burst into laughter.

"Someday he'll learn his limits," Tom said, wiping a mirthful tear from the corner of his eye. "Poor Ned."

"Poor Ned. Ha! I can't believe he doesn't know how to hold his liquor after all this time. It's not like this is new to him. I know he's been drinking in secret for at least two years," Penny said.

"At the very least," Tom said, winning a disapproving look from his mother. She then turned her attention back to Tara.

"Well, you have mastered the art of chef duty," she said. "Now we will clean up and take an extra hour to relax before continuing on with the day. Once you're ready, I'll take you out to the garden so we can do some weeding."

Tara's belly tingled with excitement at the thought of getting her hands dirty. "I look forward to it!" she said as she rose and began collecting plates with Penny. Tom rose to help her.

"Another precedence broken," Penny chimed in, and Tom flashed her an annoyed look. "We might have to keep you here forever, Tara. Suddenly my son helps with the dishes while off-duty, cleans himself up like an adult, and says nothing snarky at the table. It's like heaven." Now Tom was embarrassed beyond the realm of a natural skin color.

"I help with the dishes," he mumbled, adding to the sink pile as Penny emptied the dishwasher in preparation for a new load. She paused with a plate in her hand and patted him gently on the shoulder.

"Of course you do, Tommy. Of course you do," she said in a mockingly soothing voice before returning to her task. Tara began to scrape leftover food from the plates and rinse them to be put in the dishwasher. Tom evacuated the kitchen in an obvious attempt to prevent further embarrassment from his mother, who hummed to herself as she pressed the button to initiate the wash cycle. She recommended that Tara lie down for an hour and then change into clothes more suitable for being out in warm weather.

As she lay on her cozy bed, Tara found it strange that she already felt at home. Still, she looked forward to seeing her mother . . . and maybe even sharing this with her. Perhaps this could be their common ground.

She dozed off into an uneasy sleep.

•

Tara slid on her black funeral dress and glanced self-consciously at herself in the full-length oval mirror. She didn't much care about the ceremony, or the man of the hour for whom the funeral was being held, really.

The year before, as she was sitting in her high school biology class, she watched a plane fly into a tower in New York City. She then watched avidly with her classmates as the tower crumbled to the ground. A few of them were on cell phones, which had been loosely allowed in school again after the Columbine shooting, desperately asking about family members or friends. One school friend of Tara's sat very quiet and pale at the other end of the room. She stared at him, unsure of what to do or say.

His father was a pilot. She knew this because he was the one who flew them to Washington, D.C., for their eighth-grade field trip. He had even made a special announcement about the group on the flight, and they all cheered. His son now sat in a cloud of dread, and Tara assumed he was waiting for the call he already knew was coming. When it came, he took it quietly in the corner, hung up, and said nothing.

Finally, after staring into space for a few minutes, he rose and went up to the teacher to break the news. His father was dead. Mr. K escorted him out of the room. She hadn't seen the boy since and figured he had changed schools or something.

Sam Jr. had enlisted in the military a few months before September 11, and he was in basic training when he was informed that he would be sent to a war zone in Iraq. Tara hadn't heard much from him, though she'd heard plenty from Aunt Marilyn about what a hero he was and how hard it was to be a soldier's mother. The attention she got was too much for her to not bring it up at every possible turn.

When they got the letter that said Sam Jr. had been killed, Marilyn wailed. She'd worn fashionable black outfits for the past week, ensuring that she could mourn the death of her son in style. Tara only remembered him as the molester cousin she had done everything in her power to avoid.

She wrapped herself in a tea-length black coat and made her way to the car, where her father was waiting for her and Ali to hop in for the funeral procession.

He was buried in a small cemetery plot, though his grave was elaborate. Marilyn and Grandma Eve clung to each other, mourning their beautiful male grandchild stolen from them. Tara wondered how many other little girls he had given hickeys to . . . slept naked next to. She hoped there weren't many and was secretly glad that he would never get the chance to do either again.

The funeral passed slowly, finally coming to an uneventful end, and then everyone found themselves at Grandma Eve's kitchen table. Tara sat quietly, strategically reading a book under the table. They were supposed to be mourning the golden child, after all. Boys had always been preferred to girls, or, at the very least, to girls who didn't know their place. Tara knew where she stood in this regard. She turned a page and was surprised to find the book ripped from her hand. She looked up into her aunt's tear-stained eyes.

"You disrespectful little bitch. How dare you sneak a book in while we're mourning your cousin's death? Have some respect for your family — for this country!" she cried, ripping Tara's only copy of *Pride and Prejudice* to pieces before collapsing on the floor. Grandma Eve stooped down and placed a comforting hand on her shoulder as she glowered up at Tara with her cold blue eyes.

"Just go away, Tara. No one wants you here," Eve spat.

Tara rose and made her way to the living room.

No one wanted her here? Like that was a surprise?

"The feeling is mutual," she mumbled to herself. She wondered how to pass the time without her favorite book in hand. She sat alone in the living room for the rest of the afternoon, daydreaming about leaving and what that might be like.

•

Tara awoke with tears in her eyes again. She wondered whether she would dehydrate completely, given the excessive amount of crying going on in her sleep. She changed into a pair of shorts and a comfortable T-shirt, and headed back down to meet Penny.

It was time to put the past in her back pocket and pull some weeds.

•••

Chapter Twelve

The week passed by much more quickly than Tara had
anticipated. She was kept busy enough to almost forget about her
family issues. Still, when she lay awake at night, she would imagine just
what else she could say to her aunts to put them in their place.

For so many years, Tara was blamed for not caring enough about
the family. She was a jerk for not staying in Colorado, where it was
convenient for them to use her as they saw fit, but they were, of
course, blameless for not even bothering to consider paying her a visit.
She found out from her sister a few years ago that they had all taken a
trip to Maine to enjoy the fall foliage. She had not been contacted.

The anger and frustration that kept her from fully enjoying the
farm also gave her the fuel she needed to focus on her main goal:
going back home to Boston. In her darkest moments, she wished
deeply that she could just bring her mother with her, or that they
could have had a different life in which they lived on a private island
with immediate family only. She could have her parents, her sister,
her brother-in-law, and her beautiful nieces all to herself, and this
conflict that had defined her adult years would be resolved.

Tara held herself in check. Wishing that the past had been
different would in no way make it so, and it was something that she
carried with her forever. In essence, her past was the catalyst that led

to her future success. In the years she had been away from her
birthplace, she had fought every day to be the best at everything she
tried. She had the ghostlike image of her aunts glaring down at her in
disdain, and she used it to run that extra mile, to work on that paper
for another hour to perfect it, to fight for the best internships and the
highest credentials.

She daydreamed as she picked weed after weed after weed (the
realization that weeds were the bane of a farmer's existence had
dawned quickly) that she was ripping out her aunts' hair — their
chemically treated, dried-up, Stepford wife hair — and listened as they
screamed. She would then look up at the sky, at the mountains that
she hated or respected depending on the moment, and imagine
herself on an airplane flying home.

"You're really giving those weeds a go," Penny observed one day
as Tara was ripping each one from the ground as though she were
committing plant genocide. Tara glanced up and wiped a drop of
sweat from her brow.

"I hate weeds," she said simply. Penny just laughed. It was true. .
. . She thought that planting would be a fun experience that involved
popping seeds in the ground, watering them every so often, and then
reaping the healthy fruit soon after. But she was grossly mistaken.

"I think you find weeds annoying. I don't think it's them you're
hating right now," she observed. Tara sat up, placed a hand at her
lower back, and stretched to relieve her cramped muscles. It was
nearing four o'clock, and the sun was making its way slowly toward a
crease in the mountainside, ready to finish out the day. Penny pulled
off her thick gardening gloves and flopped them into one hand.

"Come on," she said, holding a hand out for Tara to take. "I
think you could use a drink."

Tara grabbed hold and fell in stride with Penny as they returned
to the kitchen. Penny pulled a bottle of red wine from a small black
fridge in the back corner.

"I never noticed that before," Tara observed.

"That's because if it were obvious, Ned would be hungover every day, and we'd be plum out of wine," she replied, pulling two glasses from a side cabinet and pouring a healthy dose of chardonnay in each. She hesitated for a minute before asking, "You want to talk about it?"

Tara stared at the liquid in her glass, wanting to swirl it around as though it were some kind of psychic looking glass that could show her the future, show her that she would one day be truly free. She sighed and said, "My aunts have tortured me my whole life. They look at me like I'm insane for wanting their approval, for wanting aunts who love me. It was like having two evil stepmothers, only my father was alive and simply refused to acknowledge their actions. It made it so much worse to bear knowing that he would never protect me from them." She was fighting back the mist that began to form in her eyes and took a sip of wine to numb the familiar ache.

"I'm sorry, Tara," Penny said, her voice rich with sincere sympathy. "It's always hard to face the ones we love and find that they have no capacity to love us in return. It takes a great toll, especially in the formative years, when self-confidence is either gained or lost."

"Yes, well. There's nothing I can do about it now," she sighed. "Do you know what I did before I came here? I called my aunt a . . . a goddamn lush." She stared Penny head-on, waiting for her disapproval.

"Good for you, honey," she said, taking a small sip from her own glass.

"You don't think I'm a horrible person?" Tara asked.

"Of course not! As much as I would love to believe that some magic place exists where there are only good people, I know enough to be aware that that is not the case. Good and bad exist everywhere, Tara. Sometimes people are saved from having to see the dark side of life. More often they are not. It is how we handle it, how we steer and guide our own lives in spite of the actions of others that defines who we are. It's what makes us stronger."

"I don't want to be stronger, Penny," Tara moaned, running a palm along her eyes as if that could somehow close the world out. "I want to be free. I want to be free of this place, and these people. I carry them with me every day, like a curse that I can't seem to break."

"Ah, I see. But of course you see now that they have won."

"What?" Tara asked, stunned. "They haven't won anything. They're miserable hags who are fighting old age and look like blond leather tool bags. My aunt's husband, my *uncle*, approached me for sexual favors when he was drunk. You know why I didn't spit that into her face? Because she would have found some way to twist it against me. There is no winner or loser in this situation. . . . It's all just a pile of crap." With that she clanked her glass on the table.

"That is a very true point, but you've still lost. By giving them control of your happiness, you will never be free. What you have to do is learn how to let them go, to not let them get to you. Don't you see that's how you'll hurt them the most? By not caring, by showing that they matter little to you one way or the other, you gain the upper ground. Then, if you tell yourself that you are in control of your own happiness, one day you might actually believe it."

Tara mulled that over for a minute, taking another sip of wine. Whatever vintage it was, it was smooth and delicious, and Tara felt herself relaxing. "I think you're right," she acknowledged.

"Of course I am," Penny announced. "I'm old. That's why you listen to old people — so you can figure this stuff out."

"So they say," Tara smiled. She could see where Tom had gotten his sassy sense of humor, though in the past week he hadn't shown it as openly as before. Suddenly, Tom opened the kitchen door and entered, as though her thoughts had summoned him forth. He smiled warmly at her and his mother, covered in dirt.

"Starting the party early, are we, ladies?" he asked, lifting his eyebrow as he nodded to their wine glasses.

"Who wants to know?" Penny shot back, eyeing him suspiciously from behind her goblet. "The man I see before me is a dirty stranger.

You can't possibly be my clean-cut and enjoyable son."

"No kidding. This stranger has smelled way too much goat in the past few hours. I'm going to pop in the shower real quick so dinner doesn't have eau de goat poop in it," he said before heading up the staircase to his room. Tara giggled and then checked herself. *No — stop that!* The wine wasn't helping her attraction, but somehow, once again, the little voice of warning was getting easier to ignore.

As it turned out, Tom was an amazing chef. He could grill and season chicken to perfection, and the freshly harvested vegetables tasted heavenly. With the greenhouse stocked full of spices, there was an abundance of flavor. Tara felt healthier than she had in ages and laughed heartily as Michael explained in his foreign accent the tale of his fight with the chicken coop.

"I tell yeh, they have an alliance, and it's against me in particular," he explained, going into detail of how three of the chickens (or "tree" chickens, rather) had ganged up on him when he entered the hen house and nearly pecked him a new eye socket. Nonetheless, he bravely stayed and collected the eggs, for the family's sake.

"How heroic of you, young Michael — persevering in the face of Chickengeddon," Penny joked as she cut another piece of chicken and took a bite.

"I know I wouldn't have lived to see the end of the day had it been me," Tom said in between his own laughs. Michael rolled his eyes.

"Look at this one now, fishin' for chicken-based compliments. Everyone knows you have those chickens mesmerized with yer good looks, Tommy boy. He takes one step in an' they're on their best behavior, all polite clucks. 'Please, Mr. Sanders, take my egg.' 'No, take mine!' Don't pretend like it isn't true. Yeh've cast a spell on those chickens, and it's unfair of you not to share the secret," Michael stated, pointing his fork accusingly at Tom.

Although Penny and Tara had finished their wine before dinner, Penny announced that since they had started and the following day was a day of rest, the party must continue. Tara agreed, and the two proceeded to get blotted over a few bottles of wine.

The rest of the table decided to join in as well, and Michael showed Ned how to choose and drink a proper beer, which, of course, was a Guinness. After finishing the last gulp of one with pursed lips, Ned declared that he would be changing drinks.

"Oh, no, you won't," Tom stated. "You must now suffer through Guinness for the rest of the night. Two important lessons have been learned here. One: Never listen to Michael. And two: Beer before liquor, never been sicker."

"Well, then I'll just pick another beer," Ned said, all defiance.

"Nope. House rules. How else will you truly learn your lesson?"

Ned glared him down for a full minute before huffing out a "Fine!" and grabbing another Guinness from the fridge.

"Ah, now, Ned. I think yeh'll fine tha' Guinness quickly grows on yeh. . . . It might become yer favorite beer!" Michael proclaimed.

Ned rolled his eyes and drank very slowly from his second heavy beer. The group decided that a solid round of cards was in order. They grabbed more drinks and headed into the living room. A long beige couch sat beneath whitewashed windows, its counterpart perched perpendicular to its side. A small, round oak coffee table took up the center of the room. Kaily grabbed the card game from a small shelf and set everything up.

The evening was spent in joyous merriment. Tara felt so completely alive. She leaned heavily against Penny, the two of them a picture of inebriated mirth.

"Penny," she said, slightly slurred. "I don't know how to tell you this, but I am *drunk*."

This was met with more glee. "That's okay, Tara. You just let it all out — truth-juice time!" Penny said.

"Nope," Tara said, swaying softly from side to side. "The truth has no place on this farm. No one needs to know. Shhh." She put her finger to her mouth to shush the room.

"I have a truth to say!" Kaily declared and then giggled. Her beautiful blond hair was tied up in a messy bun, and she wore sweatpants and a plain white T-shirt. Her face and spirit had an artless beauty that Tara admired and, if they were being truthful, envied just a little bit. She had immediately liked Kaily upon meeting her and was waiting in joyful anticipation of whatever announcement she wanted to make.

"I have decided to start my own farm when I get back to Canada," she announced triumphantly. Cheers and hugs erupted all around, a display of drunken delight for the ages. Penny sat forward and stretched out her arms.

"This is wonderful news, Kaily. Come hug me so I can congratulate you," she said, and Kaily tumbled across the room and fell into her motherly embrace.

They played a few rounds before everyone began to stifle their yawns. Ned had surpassed everyone and fallen asleep face-first on the long couch. A small pool of saliva had collected under his mouth.

"We could play a trick on 'im, yeh know," Michael suggested to the room. "He fell asleep wit his shoes on. Tha's a federal offense where I come from." His accent had grown broader the more he'd had to drink, and Tara had to translate his foreign English in her mind before answering.

"Nooo, we can't do that to poor Ned!" she exclaimed, rising to protect him. She nearly fell over but was caught and righted, and as she held on to the bar-like grip keeping her stable, she peered up through her hazy gaze to see Tom staring up at her.

"Oh . . . thanks, Tommy," she said with a crooked smirk. His lip curled upward as he held his ground, not letting go, and they stared at each other with goofy grins for what had to be at least a solid minute . . . or so it felt.

"Well!" Penny projected, catching the attention of the room. "I expect everyone to drink at least one full glass of water before bed so we can all avoid Ned's fate in the morning. No hangovers for us seasoned adults, eh?"

"I've been drinking since I was eighteen," Kaily announced proudly. "I can hold my liquor better than anyone!"

"Yeah, right," Michael murmured. "No one can match an Irishman for drink, especially not a Canadian!"

"I am a farmer! I'm tough as nails," Kaily retorted. "Now, if you'll *excuse* me, I shall retire."

In a grand style, she led the way to the staircase opposite of Tara's and held tight to the railing as she made her way up.

"After you, sir," Penny said to Michael, falling in line behind him. She glanced back, unable to resist.

"Don't stay up too late now, lovebirds," she yelled before disappearing from sight.

It was then Tara realized in her clouded mind that Tom still had his arms wrapped around her, and she was suddenly very aware of his chest pressing into her back.

"Oops," she said, fumbling to stand on her own so he wouldn't keep holding her. This proved to be a challenge, and Tom had to hold her forearms to steady her before she finally stood upright without help.

"Why aren't you funny anymore, Tom?" Tara asked bluntly.

"What?" he asked.

"I *said*, 'Why aren't you funny anymore?' When we first met, you were hilarious. Now it's like you never know what to say." His eyes flashed, as though he were being hunted. To Tara's muddled surprise, he almost looked scared of her.

"It's just . . . there's something I have to tell you . . . something I probably should have told you a long time ago."

"Ahh, truuuth juice," Tara said.

"Yeah, well . . . I dunno. Maybe you shouldn't know."

"Are you serious? You bring up a dreaded secret that involves me and then tell me you're not going to spit it out? I will kick you right in the shin." She feigned a kick and nearly fell over again. Tom once again helped her upright.

"I knew your mother before I knew you," he blurted. Tara removed herself from his reach.

"So? Not to burst your bubble, Tom, but I already knew that tender piece of information. You're cleared."

"She asked me to fly to Boston the day you were to fly out here and find you at the airport."

This stopped her cold. Her mother sent him to the airport? For what purpose? Was this another game she was playing to get Tara to see things her way?

Tara thought back to that day at the airport. Tom had clung to her, taking up her time, following her to the airplane. For the first time, she realized that it could have all been an act.

Her head was spinning, the liquor burning through her veins as her temples began to throb with the effort to think clearly.

"Why did you go?" she asked, her expression cold.

She wanted answers. She wanted to believe that Tom was apart from everything that was bad in her life. He was meant to be the one untainted thing. Why was he ruining that?

"Because I wanted to help her. She's dying, Tara . . ."

"Yes, I am perfectly aware that my mother is dying, thank you," she snipped. She would not be told about her own mother by this half-stranger. What did he know?

"I know, I know. I'm sorry," he said, putting his hands up in defense from her wrath. "It's just that I wanted to help her, but I also felt so strange when I saw your picture. I wanted to find you. I wanted to help you feel better about this place. So I flew out and waited for you, and suddenly there you were, and I thought . . ."

"You thought, 'Hey, let's charm this girl out of hating her home and family so I can manipulate her into staying.' Right?"

His face turned stern. "No. I thought, 'If I die tomorrow, I'll be glad to know that my heart could actually beat this way for another human being.'"

She sat in stunned silence. Truth juice indeed. . . . Was he so shy because he had some semblance of love for her? She had laughed off his mother's jokes and his open embarrassment, but she hadn't actually considered the possibility that she was dead-on about his feelings. She rose from the sofa as he slowly, achingly slowly, stepped closer and cupped her face in his hands. He kissed her softly, as though pressing any harder would break her. She kissed him back instinctively, increasing the pressure and letting him know that she was stronger than he knew. The implications of his confession took a back seat to an instant carnal lust. In fact, Tara found herself forgetting what he had just said altogether.

She pulled away from him, her eyes shining with liquor and passion, and took his hand. They made their way up upstairs to her bed, and it was there she made love to Tom Sanders for the very first time.

● ● ●

Chapter Thirteen

Tara blinked once, twice.

Her mouth was bone-dry, a desperate need for water the first discernable thought to fully form in her muddled mind. She cracked one eye open and immediately closed it, moaned, and went to roll over.

But something was behind her in the way. Slowly blinking her eyes back open, she looked down and found a hairy arm looped around her middle. She followed the arm to its origin and winced as her gaze landed on Tom's face.

"Oh, no, no, nooo," she groaned as she buried her head into the pillow. Tom began to stir, and he retrieved his arm and attempted to sit up.

"Holy God. . . . The room — why is it still spinning?!" he asked, lying back down and pulling his hands over his eyes as if to rub the sensations away. A minute later, he slowly removed his hands from his eyes and stared sheepishly at Tara, who peeked back at him from her vantage point between the pillows.

He smirked.

"Oops," he said, squinting through his clouded vision. Tara smirked back.

"Oops," she agreed. Rolling over to her side and propping her head delicately on her hand, she tried her best to ignore the thirst that still plagued her.

"So . . . how much of last night do you remember?" she asked. *This could be very, very bad. Or it could be great. Really could go either way at this point,* she thought. Tom scrunched up his face, resembling a young child looking for the answer to a hard math problem. He then began to piece the night back together.

"We were playing games. . . . You were terrible, if I recall correctly."

"That is false. I'm pretty sure I won the game," Tara retorted.

"Nevertheless," he continued, "there was some sort of dancing and merriment, and then suddenly, everyone was gone, and we were dancing . . . in the moonlight . . . feelin' warm and right . . . " His voice drifted off, and he smiled at her.

"We weren't dancing. I got pushed over or something, and then somehow you showed up behind me."

"Exactly, because we were daaaancin' in the moonlight." He began to croon the lyrics to the old song, resulting in a throw pillow launched at his head. He ducked and dove down into a position where he was once again holding Tara in his arms.

Okay, might as well, Tara thought, and she snuggled into his chest. A patch of black hair covered his upper body and thinned out into a narrow trail past his navel. As her thoughts journeyed south of that spot, she shook her head, again directing her focus to the night that had led to such a precarious situation.

"So then what happened?" she asked, hoping Tom would have a better drunken memory than she did. He began to gently stroke her hair as he rested his chin on top of her head. He thought for a few seconds.

"I think I bruised myself coming up the stairs," he said, lifting his left leg out from under the blankets for confirmation.

"Yep, that's proof of that," he said, admiring the nasty bruise on his shin. "Probably saving you from certain death, I imagine." He moved his hands down to squeeze her middle playfully. Tara gently tugged his hands away, not wanting to be distracted.

"Yeah, right," she said. "Do continue the retelling. We need some Sherlock Holmes business up in here right now."

"Right. So we made it back here. . . . I remember kissing, maybe a warm cloud of heavenly awesomeness, and then . . ."

He kissed the top of her head.

"And then?" Tara prompted.

"Well, I should think the rest is pretty self-explanatory," he said.

"You're really excited about this, aren't you?" she asked incredulously. He shrugged.

"Excited to wake up in bed with a lovely young woman who also happens to have a great sense of humor and a strong work ethic? I'd say so." He gave her a small squeeze. Suddenly, Tara felt cold. She pushed away from him a little bit so she could look him in the eye. His gaze went from content to nervous in seconds.

"Tom . . .," she started, not knowing what to say. "You know that my time here . . . it's not permanent. My mom doesn't have much time, and after she passes, I'll be going back home as soon as I can. The most we could hope for in this situation is maybe a summer fling that can bring us fond memories later on. Otherwise, I would chalk this night up to mistakes and pretend it didn't happen." The disappointment on his handsome face made her want to cry.

If only things could be different . . .

But they weren't. His home was here; hers was there; and there was nothing that could change the way she felt about it. She watched his face as he struggled to control his emotions before he finally sighed and pulled her back into his arms. His body was tense.

"Well, I think I'd like option A, if that's quite all right with you," he said. She was hoping he would say that. She hadn't been able to touch a man, be with a man, in ages, and what could be bad about adding a summer romance to her life? It would certainly be a first in her book, and something she had always wanted to experience. She began to rub his back to loosen him up, and she felt him begin to relax.

"Well then," she said coyly. "I suppose we should see what we've got to work with here, maybe in a capacity we will actually remember afterward."

"I do think it would be better if we saw each other naked — you know, just for full disclosure," he said, a wolfish grin replacing his disappointment.

"We can do that as soon as you bring me Advil and a very tall drink of water, or I'm telling you right now that I won't be at my best."

"Okay, let's give ourselves a nice day of recovery, and we'll see where we end up tonight."

"I couldn't agree more." She was excited to quench her unquenchable thirst in more ways than one. The day was spent in sweatpants, as the entire household had, at some point or another, stumbled down the stairs with their hair piled on one side of their head or one pant leg up. In the warmth of the early afternoon, they all took refuge in the shade of a large willow tree. Penny was kind enough to throw a few futon cushions out and pack a cooler full of beverages designed to help hangovers.

Penny was as sprightly and energetic as ever, which made her ridiculing her son and the staff all the more aggravating. She teased and taunted every one of them until Tom took Tara's example and threw a pillow in Penny's general direction. It landed flat on the ground in front of her, and her laugher rang out into the fields.

"You're all lucky this is a rest day," she crowed. "Otherwise I'd have you puking in the bush before letting you off the clock. Farm life is tough, you know." She chuckled, ignoring the moans.

Tara leaned back on one of the pillows and gazed up at the thousands of veined leaves swirling around in the breeze. She had decided that sleeping with Tom had been a bad idea. She had managed to complicate an already overwhelming situation, and only in her first week on the job. Way to go, Tara. As great as a summer romance seemed in her imagination, the reality of leaving it behind was sobering.

"This seat taken?" she heard Tom's weary voice ask. She said nothing and, with her eyes closed, patted the space next to her in invitation. She felt his heavy body sink into the cushion. He took her hand in his, and they laid there in the summer warmth. For a while they said nothing and simply absorbed the peacefulness of nature's silence. The warm breeze blew over her inert body, and she took a deep breath. The world was still, and the earth beneath her was slowly nurturing its unborn plants. She felt her complicated life begin to grow calm. Finally, Tom spoke.

"I don't want to complicate your life, Tara," he said, as though he had been reading her mind moments before. "I like spending time with you. I like how I feel when I'm with you. If you'd be willing to enjoy what little time we do have this summer, I would be grateful to be a part of your life, even for just one chapter of it."

Tara pondered for a minute. Tom had done everything to try and show her that she had value, that she was a worthy and beautiful woman. Time after time she had refused to believe him and pushed his comments aside — just more empty words. In that moment, she really looked at him and considered what he had to say. It really was quite perfect: a summer on a farm, having amazing sex with a beautiful, kind-hearted man. In that moment, under the willow tree, she turned her body inward to face his and placed a gentle, accepting kiss on his lips.

"That sounds wonderful, Tom Sanders," she said. He hugged her briefly before letting her sink back into her original position.

"Oh, by the way," he said, "your parents and sister and nieces are coming over for dinner tonight."

Tara opened her eyes. "My family?"

"Yes," he confirmed. "Your mom was a little worried, since you looked so nervous at your last parting. She's decided to come up every weekend in summer, while it's still nice."

"That will be wonderful. Thank you," she said, smiling warmly at him.

"Anything for my summer romance," he said with a wink. He rolled back over and closed his eyes, and they slept peacefully in the shade, their hands still clasped together.

Dinner was a wild affair, complete with food fights, drinking contests, and uncontained laughter. Of course, the drinking contests were held with water, since most of the group had made a vow to never drink again.

Maddie was entertained by Michael's accent and the way he pronounced his words. When they began counting together and he said "tree," she giggled and mimicked him, singing "One, two, tree! One, two, tree!" over and over again.

Emily was cradled in Tara's lap, content to spend time in the arms of her aunt. Her eyes glowed as she enjoyed the shenanigans going on around her, and a sense of peace was brought to Tara's heart holding her.

Claire seemed in good form, though Tara noted how tired she looked. It seemed she'd lost more weight every time Tara saw her, and the woman had no more weight to lose. Still, she seemed content as she gazed around the table, glad to have her family in close vicinity. Tara's father chatted with Kaily about Canadian politics and business, which she had a fair knowledge of because of her father's company. In fact, it was the business world that had driven Kaily to farm life, as the cutthroat atmosphere had been overwhelming and disheartening.

Tom had cooked steak and potatoes with some fresh peas. It was, quite frankly, the best meal Tara had ever had. After spending a lazy day together, the cloud of alcohol had lifted from her mind, and she found herself feeling comfortable in this situation. Her mother looked at Tom with open adoration, and in that moment Tara remembered Tom's confession that Claire had sent him on her own behalf. A wave of frustration battled with her sense of contentment. Even when Tara thought she had found someone she could enjoy, her mother had still somehow managed to manipulate the situation. No matter what Tara did, it was as though she would never be free of her mother's grasp.

Glancing across the table, she eyed her mother's wiry frame and wondered just how much of an influence she had in her current romance. The longer she had been on the farm, the more she had managed to stave off memories of her past, but as she considered the numerous times her mother had overstepped, crossed boundaries she shouldn't have . . .

Tara took a breath and tried to let the past be. She knew that she would never have a chance to heal if she were to let her anger flare up every time her mother acted inappropriately. With so little time left with her, Tara did her best to release and forgive, fighting to stay in the present.

She was surrounded by good food, laughter, and friendship. At the end of the meal, someone halfheartedly suggested game night. Tara looked around the table at her slumped down, overly exhausted comrades. It was certainly no time for games — not after last night's shenanigans. Her mother begged a polite exit, making the excuse that the girls needed to get home and be put to bed. They made their way out to the cars, and Tara stroked Emily's delicate peach-colored cheek before strapping her into her car seat.

"Maddie, say goodbye to Auntie Tara," Ali cajoled. Maddie waddled with her hands at her sides over to Tara, who knelt down to be at her level. The child leaned into Tara and waited for her to wrap her arms around her. Tara couldn't help but laugh.

"Oh, I see. The girl just expects to be hugged, does she?"

"She does tend to get VIP treatment," Ali joked. As Tara closed Emily in, Maddie walked back over and took her mother's hand before being lifted into her own toddler seat. Once all car doors were closed and seat belts were buckled, Tara waved as her family drove off into the fading dusk.

Penny and Tara took up the task of cleaning up the kitchen. Tom sat with his head on the dining room table.

"Did I mention I'm never drinking again?" he mumbled into the wood.

"If I had a nickel for every time I've heard that around here . . .," Penny replied. She placed the last dish into the dishwasher and set it to wash. She then put a hand on Tara's shoulder and gestured toward the staircase. "Off you go, now. We actually have to get to working from here on out, so I hope you all enjoyed your last day of relaxation!"

Tara glared playfully at Penny but said nothing. She shook her head, bade her goodnight, and trudged up the stairs.

Feeling disgusting, she dragged herself into the bathroom to take a quick shower. She relished in the warm water on her booze-ravaged body and very much looked forward to a night of beautiful, buzz-free sleep. She made short work of dressing in comfortable sweatpants and a black tank top before sliding into bed, her body sinking blissfully into the mattress.

She sighed. Sleeping alone wasn't exactly ideal, and she stared at the door, willing him to enter. After about ten minutes of waiting, she was rewarded.

Tom knocked lightly on the door and opened it a crack before coming in.

"Visitors accepted?" he asked in a hushed tone.

"Gratefully accepted," she replied. She scooted over to make room. He slid in beside her, took her up in a gentle embrace, and held her close. She waited for him to make a move . . . to initiate sex they might both actually remember . . . until she heard a small snore. Tom Sanders had fallen fast asleep.

Amused, she snuggled into him and found that she could no longer keep her eyes open either. She fell into the depths of the unconscious, not heeding anything but the blissful nature of sleep after a long discomfort.

•••

Chapter Fourteen

It was a conversation Tara had imagined so many times, a story her mother had told her. Her twenty-seven-year-old father, Bob, sat in his parents' kitchen and stared into space.

•

Two girls, he thought. What was he going to be able to do with two girls? What would happen when they got older, when they expected things from him he didn't know how to give? His father, Jon, walked into the room, his jet-black hair and bright-blue eyes showcasing what a vibrant and healthy man he was. Bob loved his father; he respected him more than anyone else.

"What brings you in, son?" Jon asked kindly. Bob was his eldest and smartest son, and he had done his damn best to make sure he was a man who could provide for himself and, of course, a family — hopefully a boy, to carry on the family name. Jon knew that the ultrasound had predicted a girl, but they had been known to be wrong from time to time.

"It's a girl, Dad. We named her Tara Ann," he said softly. Jon said nothing. He knew his other son would never attract a woman to marry, let alone reproduce, and Claire was stern in only wanting two. His name would die with his sons now.

"Aren't you going to congratulate me?" Bob asked. Really he was looking for some kind of advice on how to be a parent. Ali had been an easy baby, and Claire had taken over that department nicely. Now, with two babies, it was harder for her to keep up, and he didn't know how to rise to the task himself.

"Of course," Jon said gruffly, trying to swallow his disappointment. He joined his son at the table, sitting across from him. "Give my best to little Taryn."

"It's Tara," Bob said stiffly.

"Yes, of course it is." Jon waved his hand dismissively. They sat in silence for a while, lost in their own thoughts.

"What do I do, Dad?" Bob finally asked, running a hand through his already thinning brown hair. Jon gave him a quizzical glance.

"What do you mean, what do you do? You're a father now, Bob. Your job isn't to be their friend; it's to make money and protect them. They're girls, so they'll be even more of a hassle."

Bob sighed. He had grown up with two wild sisters, and he knew what girls could be like. Even though Claire had a maturity and a strength that belied her years, he still didn't know what he would do with his children. Had they been boys, he could have gone camping with them, taught them to ride motocross or anything athletic. Now his job would be much more challenging: He would have to keep them safe from the rest of the world.

Long before he and Claire hopped in his old truck and drove to Vegas to get married, Bob had been a wild child. He'd spent his nights playing drinking games with his friends, and shooting out streetlights with BB guns and never getting caught. There had been no end to his mischief until Claire became his wife. His father had ingrained in him the need to provide, and so, he began working at his company immediately. He learned the world of computers and became good at it. No matter how hard the challenge, he found a way to financially support his new family.

His family of girls. How would he ever be able to relate to them? He would leave the emotional rearing to Claire while he worked to ensure they could get the best education possible, have the things they wanted out of life. He did love them, of course. He was a twenty-seven-year-old man who had no idea what to do with his children. Was that so uncommon?

"Thanks for the advice, Dad," Bob said, rising from his chair. "I'd better get back. . . . I've got some work to get started on." Jon rose and patted his son firmly on the back.

"There's a good man," he said. He walked him toward the door. "We'll see you real soon to meet the baby . . . er, Tamera."

"For God's sake, Dad, her name is Tara. Whatever her gender, her grandparents had better at least know her damn name."

"Of course," Jon laughed. "We'll get it someday."

Once Bob left, Jon made his way back to the bedroom, where Eve was lounging on their bed and watching TV.

"Was that Bob?" she asked, her back propped against the headboard as she popped a piece of toast into her mouth. It was still morning, and she had yet to change out of her floral nightgown. She didn't look away from the television as she spoke to her husband.

"Yep," Jon replied. "Turns out they had another girl. Named her Tara or Turin or something."

Eve frowned, prying her eyes from the screen and staring at Jon. "Another girl?"

"Yep."

"Well," she said. "I guess we'll just have to put up with it."

"Guess so." Jon couldn't even muster excitement about meeting the child for the first time, and he didn't bother worrying about it.

Such a disappointment.

•

Tara blinked. The sun entered the room through her open window, beams of light caressing her face. She moved to stretch and felt Tom's hand slowly move up toward her breast. As she turned in the circle of his arms, she met his gaze and saw unrestrained passion. He claimed her lips in a fierce kiss, and she clung to him, hungry for more.

It was so much better than she remembered. Tom was gentleness and excitement and passion all in one, a cocktail Tara craved. They explored each other in the gentle morning light, their bodies coming together as they reached the heights of ecstasy. As their euphoria subsided, Tom curled himself around Tara, kissing her temple as he nestled his chin against her head.

Tara's stomach growled, and Tom laughed.

"I like a girl with a hearty appetite," he said. Tara chuckled.

"Then you've found the right one."

"I think so," Tom replied. Tara's heart fluttered at the double meaning of his words. She fought to control her own emotions as she shifted slightly away to look up at him.

"Time for breakfast, then?"

Tom kissed the tip of her nose.

"Absolutely."

The month of June seemed to pass by in a blink. Tara fell into a regular routine: planting in the garden, weeding, weeding, and weeding. She became friends with the goats and chickens; she gave them names and watched with amusement as they really did obey everything Tom asked of them.

"You see," Michael said one day, "he seduces any hen in a hundred-mile radius. The man is a chicken Casanova." He shook his head as he headed for the orchards to do some trimming.

Tara had wondered for a while whether she and Tom were being too obvious with each other. He had spent every night in her bed since that drunken night, and their time together had become better and better. It was clear that the others sensed something was going on between them, and to her relief, no one asked any questions. It was as though their relationship was allowed to be kept a public secret, respected privacy that everyone knew about, which suited Tara just fine. She had no intention of being secretive, especially not among those who she had come to know as good friends. Out in the middle of the Rocky Mountains with no screen time, she had learned to enjoy life in the old way: telling stories and playing games. Michael could play the piano, Kaily the guitar, and between them there were many nights of horrifically off-key musical numbers.

One thing remained consistent, and that was the small knock on Tara's door every night. Tom would sneak in, and they would spend hours making love, talking, or simply being in the same space together. Tara told him some of her childhood stories and all the reasons she had wanted so badly to leave. He opened up about how his father had died — suddenly and without warning. He lost him when he was sixteen, and took his place working the farm and keeping it alive.

The whole town had mourned the death of Billy Sanders. He was an active member of the community and a beloved father and husband. He raised funds for the poor and donated any extra food he could to shelters in Denver.

"He always said that everyone deserved a healthy, fresh meal," Tom explained in the deep quiet of the night, holding Tara tightly as he recalled his most pleasant memories of his father. Tara lay still and allowed him to tell his tale uninterrupted.

"One night, he was driving back up from Denver. I guess it was a prom night," he said bitterly. "A car full of drunken teens swerved onto his path. . . . The police report stated that he tried to avoid them and drove right into a ditch. He died instantly."

Tara turned in the circle of his arms and stared up into the shadows on his face. Knowing that nothing could be said that would be sufficient, she settled for stroking his cheek in sympathy. He placed his hand on hers and squeezed it gently in acknowledgement.

"I wish that I didn't know what loss felt like," he said sadly. She sighed.

"I wish that, too. When it piles up so high, you wonder how you'll survive it, how to live every day with just a little bit less of yourself. You try to find out how to let go."

"You found one way to do it, Tara," he said. "By running away."

She tensed.

"I didn't *run away*, Tom. I ran home."

"Did you?"

She pushed away from him, rolled to the other side of the bed, and faced her back to him.

"I did," she said tersely. "We should get some sleep. We have a lot of work to do tomorrow." He was silent for a moment. She felt him sigh before turning his back to her.

"We certainly do," he said quietly.

And the subject was closed once again.

Tom did not bring up Tara's status as a runaway-turned-fugitive-of-her-mother's-illness again, and she was glad. Just because they were sleeping together did not give him the right to evaluate what she should or shouldn't do with her own life, she reasoned. But deep down, she knew that she just did not want to face the truth of his words. She rolled over and closed her eyes, determined to release her negative feelings into the void, at least for now.

July was approaching quickly, and the strawberries would need to be readied for the strawberry festival. Tara was excited to be a part of what was looking to be a joyous and entertaining affair. Penny enlisted the help of face painters and balloon artists. She had a local baker lined up to facilitate a strawberry cupcake walk, which, from what Tara could understand, was like musical chairs that ended with a cupcake for the winner. Tara's family came up and celebrated the Fourth of July on the farm, her father's car laden with illegal fireworks from Wyoming.

As a child, Tara found it impossible to believe that her father could be the troublemaker her mother said he was. But now she could see that the quiet, stoic man she usually knew had a wild side, and it usually manifested in some form of activity with explosives.

They pulled out some wooden foldout chairs and laid out blankets for Ali, Harold, and the babies. Bob started lighting off some sparklers that dazzled Maddie, but little Emily remained asleep in her mother's lap, clearly unimpressed. Tom cooked up hamburgers and hot dogs, and they all enjoyed Claire's potato salad and blueberry tarts.

Tara took a sip of her favorite beer, a smooth Boston summer ale. The cool liquid bubbled on her tongue and danced its way down her throat, giving her that perfect contrast of hot and cold. The sky had been a brilliant blue all day, and as dusk fell, it turned into a wavy indigo. Penny turned on a few house lights, but the only other lighting came from the brilliant bursts of sparks Bob was gleefully setting off one by one. Tara gazed thoughtfully at her family — her mother curled up in a soft chair, her sister keeping a watchful eye on Maddie, who looked eager to touch the magic lights in the sky and be with her grandpa as he made them come to life. She felt a strange sense of nostalgia, as though she were missing something that she'd never actually had.

She walked over and sat at the base of Claire's chair. She began stroking Tara's hair.

"Tara, there's something that I need to tell you," she declared as she pulled Tara's long hair from her ponytail and tugged out strands to begin a French braid. Tara tilted her head back and closed her eyes, enjoying the feeling of being groomed.

"Mm?" was all she said. Claire's hands worked meticulously, pulling gently at tangles and collecting errant strands.

She really is a wizard with hair, Tara thought idly.

"I've stopped taking any treatment."

Tara stiffened and took the words in. She slowly pulled away so she could turn around and face her mother. Claire released her hair and regarded her with quiet resignation.

"Why?" Tara whispered, as though doing so would prevent the children from hearing her. Like they would even understand at such a tender young age. Claire sighed.

"It's not working anyway, honey. You know how I feel about prolonging this kind of thing, after everything we went through with your grandfather."

Tara grasped her mother's hand and pressed her forehead against it, trying to somehow will the disease to freeze in its place, stop it from thinning her mother out from her very core. She could feel her eyes filling up with tears.

"Did I run away from home, Mom?" she asked timidly, once again that shy little girl who couldn't understand why no one liked her. Claire took Tara's hand and placed a small kiss on it before resting it in her lap.

"You went where you needed to go, I suppose. I still wish you had been in touch more often."

"You didn't want me to be in touch. You wanted me to always be here." It was a fact, not an opinion. Claire sighed.

"I did want you here — against my better judgment. I believed that your aunts would eventually grow up and treat you better, or that you would find a way to ignore them."

Tara sat in silence. Her mother had expedited her own demise, and there was no knowing how soon it would come.

"Maybe I should go home with you," Tara said.

"You don't need to do that, Tara . . ."

"How much time do we have left, Mom? I want to spend it with you." Her tears spilled out freely. She could feel her father casting glances in their direction.

"I think that sounds wonderful, Tara," Claire said, calm as a cucumber, "but you're not coming home with me."

"Why?!" Tara asked. It made no sense that her mother would deny her the chance to spend their last weeks together, after everything they had been through.

"Because she's staying with us," Tom said from behind her. Tara turned quickly and tilted her head up to see him clearly. He was somber. She felt Claire squeeze her hand in reassurance, but she stared at Tom in disbelief.

"Oh, now don't blame Tommy, Tara. I called him a day or two ago and made the request myself. All he did was provide an answer and then — against his will, I assure you — promise to not say anything until I could tell you myself." Tara made a point to remove the likely blame-filled expression from her face, returning her attention back to her mother.

"You want to stay with me?" she asked quietly. She was pleased and amazed at the same time. Claire waved her hand nonchalantly.

"No, I want to live out my days in the beautiful countryside, enjoying the peacefulness of nature. Having you here is just a fun bonus," she said with a smirk.

"Ah," Tara said. Bob made his way over to their small party and lay a hand on Tara's head.

"What can we do, squirt? No one can say no to your mother these days, and she takes full advantage of that," he said, gazing lovingly down at Claire, who returned the look in kind.

"Damn right I do," Claire said. "Now go bring our things to Tommy's extra room, Bob. I'd like to spend the rest of the evening with my girls." Bob nodded and patted Tara's head once more before heading off. That was about as affectionate as he had ever been with her. She was flush with the new sensation of filial attention. Tom immediately offered to help him get settled, and Harold followed, not knowing what else to do. Maddie toddled her way over, holding tightly to Ali's hand and trying to pull her along.

"Gamma, Gamma!" she cried out, falling into Tara's lap in her attempt to reach Claire. Her mother let out a rich, throaty laugh and pulled Maddie up.

"Did you like the fireworks?" she asked. Maddie nodded in affirmation. She had finagled a pacifier from Ali, a comfort object that was in the process of being weaned out when there weren't people around to hear the tantrums. They began playing various games involving toes and noses and were oblivious to the rest of the world. Ali plopped down beside Tara and gazed out at the mountainous landscape around them. She crossed her legs, leaned back against Claire's sturdy wooden chair, and glanced sideways at Tara.

"What was all that about?" she asked quietly.

"What did you hear?" Tara questioned in return.

"That Mom's coming out here until . . ." She couldn't find the will to finish the sentence. They all wanted so desperately to avoid the subject — well, everyone except Claire, of course.

"Yes," Tara interrupted.

"Are you okay with that?" Ali asked.

"Why wouldn't I be? We're finally in a place where I can be myself around her," she said, pausing in surprise at her own words. Could she really be herself here? She was a stone's throw from *those* people, and yet up here, she somehow felt a force field around her. Having been in good company and able to laugh freely without being judged, she had finally begun to feel safe.

"What if Marilyn or Jo come up to see Dad?" Ali asked. Tara thought, staring out in the general direction her sister had moments before.

"We'll figure it out when the time comes," Claire chimed in. Clearly, she was not as oblivious as they had thought. Ali smiled softly, but there was worry behind her eyes that she couldn't hide.

Tara spent the rest of the night allowing baby Emily to clutch her finger; she was amazed at the strength of the newborn's grip. They all chatted and made plans for Ali and the girls to come up the following weekend for the strawberry festival — and, most likely, every weekend after that.

Bob, Tom, and Harold returned to the little party after a short while, and as the night grew darker, Maddie's head steadily began to droop; it seemed she would fall asleep upright any minute, her head

teetering back and forth. Ali carefully lifted her, Harold took Emily in
his arms, and they said their goodbyes under the porch light of the
purple farmhouse. Claire and Bob made their way back inside with
Penny, who had been inside cleaning up, or, more accurately, giving
the Kingston family their own space to be with one another. She
showed Claire and Tara the new guest room, which was off the
kitchen down a hallway that Tara hadn't noticed before.

"It's just perfect," Claire said, giving Penny a hug.

"I'm glad you like it. I knew having a room on the first floor
would come in handy at some point. Tomorrow I'll show you where
the laundry is, and all that logistical mumbo jumbo."

"That will be wonderful," Claire said. She stifled a yawn with one
hand and squeezed Penny's hand with the other. "Thanks again,
Penny. You don't know what this means to us."

"Oh, I think I have some idea." She slyly winked at Claire and
then turned to head back toward the kitchen with Tara. Tara gave her
mother a quick hug goodnight and waved to her father just as he
closed the door behind her. Not exactly the social butterfly, as always.

Unable to hold back her own massive yawn, Tara excused herself
and made her way upstairs. She hadn't noticed where Tom had
disappeared off to, and she wondered whether he would show up in
her room given her subtle display of blame earlier. As she reached the
top of the staircase, she noticed her door was slightly ajar, a warm light
flickering from behind the small slit. She slowly pressed it open to
reveal two tall candlesticks on either side of her bed and Tom sitting
on the edge of the bed, waiting for her arrival.

"Is it our anniversary?" she asked, crossing her arms. He looked
nervous, like he had been practicing what to say over and over again.
He stood and made his way over to her. He didn't touch her, but he
was standing close enough for her to feel his nervous energy like a
pulse.

"It's more like an apology. I know I shouldn't have interfered with your family's things. It's just that your mother was so convincing, and I didn't know what else to do . . ."

Tara put her hand on his mouth to get him to stop rambling. "I know how my mother is, trust me. You don't need to feel bad, Tom. I do. At the first opportunity, I wanted to be angry with you. I wanted you to be at fault."

He stared at her, bewildered. "Why?"

She paused and considered her answer. Finally, she said, "Because if I don't, I'm in danger of falling deeply in love with you."

"Then will you accept my apology wine party?" he asked without skipping a beat. She laughed. It was amazing that he could just blow by her statement so easily.

"I thought I told you that you didn't need to apologize." He ran the back of his fingers along her temples and smoothed some wisps of hair behind her ears. A fierce intensity was present in his eyes.

"I do, actually." He took her hand and led her over to the bed, where two glasses of merlot sat on the bedside table. "You see, I've already fallen in love with you."

●●●

Chapter Fifteen

With her parents' presence nearby, the floodgate to Tara's memories was opened once again.

Tara crouched behind a wall and listened to her mother cry.

Claire sat at Gran's kitchen table, devastated. She sniffed back a sob and wiped her face angrily as another tear dropped from the corner of her left eye. Alice brought her old teapot and delicate cups to the table and poured for the two of them before taking a seat right next to Claire. She put her hand on her daughter's in comfort.

"I'm a terrible mother," Claire whispered. "What have I let happen to my little girls?"

"You're a wonderful mother. You can't protect them from everything," Alice said soothingly.

"They never liked going there, you know," Claire said bitterly. "But I ignored them. I thought they just missed us . . ." She let a sob loose and held a tissue to her mouth and nose to hide the sight of her crumbling confidence.

She had believed that she was a good mother. Her girls were kind-hearted, and they never talked back to her or Bob. She had raised them to be ambitious and smart, both streetwise and scholastically — at least she had thought so, until the day she and Bob returned from their trip to find their daughters' necks marked up and down by their cousin's mouth. She didn't dare imagine what else he had done, what it had felt like for them to let him subject them to it. When she went over to Jon and Eve's to berate them for letting this happen, they were unrepentant.

"We raised four children, Claire. I think we know what we're doing" was all Eve had to say in reply to her accusations. Bob was furious. He stormed over to Marilyn's house, cuffed the ingrate on the head, and threatened to neuter him if he ever touched their girls again. That night, they lay in bed together in shock. They felt like failures. The girls seemed fine, but the guilt was so heavy it was crushing them both.

"Claire, you're going to do everything you can to keep your children safe; you're going to fight like hell to prevent them from knowing what the world can be, how horrible it can be. You'll never succeed, and if you lock them away, they'll only find a worse way out for themselves."

"But how do we move on? How do we move past this knowing we're going to have to see that little shit every damn week?"

"You do it just like we always do . . . persevere in silence with a watchful eye. If Bob insists that you still see his family so often, then it's the only solution you've got."

"You think I can?" Claire asked, her eyes wide as she stared up at her mother with unshed tears stuck to moist lashes. She knew if anyone could give her faith in herself, it was her mother. She was the only one who knew just what to say and how to say it. She was the only who could make Tara smile, for which Claire was grateful. It was deeply saddening to see her daughter frowning almost constantly, but with Bob's connection to his family, Claire felt helpless to do anything about it. She couldn't ask him to drop his relatives any more than he could ask her to stop talking to her mother.

"I've never known anyone who could be stronger for her family than you, Claire," Alice reassured. Although it didn't make the guilt go away, it made her smile just a teensy, tiny bit. It would have to suffice for the moment.

"I love them more than life itself, Mom," Claire stated firmly. Alice held her daughter's watery gaze.

"No one knows that more than me. You hold that thought close to you, use it as your guiding light, and you'll come out of this. You all will."

Claire sighed. "I hope so. Something tells me we'll lose Tara, and I won't know what I'll do when the day comes."

"You'll love her," Claire replied. "It's all you can ever do."

Summer continued to slide by like a warm, lazy river. Tara spent her days in the garden with her mother and Penny, laughing and whittling away the hours. Tom had taken Bob under his wing; the old man had his work cut out for him with the larger crops, though he seemed to enjoy working with his hands in nature. During the few weeks preceding the festival, Tara felt a complete and unfamiliar peace.

The strawberry festival arrived, and people from all around the state made their way to the purple farmhouse to pick berries and try some of the delicious confections baked by Penny and Claire. The strawberry cupcake walk was a huge success, and visitors and farmhands alike filled themselves up with sweet fruit and cool cream. Kennedy had driven up in her pink Volkswagen Beetle to spend the day with the family, and her company was refreshing. Her youthful exuberance revealed none of her mother's nasty and controlling behavior, and for that Tara couldn't have been happier.

Tara watched as her father lifted Maddie onto his broad shoulders and snuck her strawberries. She looked around to see if Ali might be somewhere ready to protest, but she was busy chatting with Harold at one of the picnic tables. They were glad to have a break to be together as a couple, rather than as parents.

Once the festival was over, the harvest became a much larger task. Tara often worked the farm stand at the market with Kaily, and Tom was never far from her side.

After his confession, Tara hadn't really been sure what to do with their situation. He hadn't expected her to say that she loved him back, though she had pretty much already admitted to it. Still, sometimes when she was knee-deep in dirt scraping off vegetables, she found herself thinking about going back home. Without treatment, Claire's condition was getting worse every day. While she had once been able to stand at the market alongside her daughter, she now stayed home with Penny, who looked after her diligently alongside Bob.

Walking was becoming difficult for Claire. She spent most of her time sitting in a rocking chair overlooking the farm and mountainside with a nice homemade quilt on her lap. Tara watched her sometimes when she got home, before Claire noticed her presence. She looked peaceful, as though she were accepting of her life and glad of it. Tara hoped that she could face the end of her own life with such calm maturity.

Having returned from another shift at the market, she strode over, pulled up a chair beside Claire, and gazed out at the hard work they had done. It was beautiful.

"You have a good turnout today?" Claire asked.

"Same as usual, really. We have a lot of good regulars around here."

"That's good. Good." She slowly rocked back and forth. Finally, she turned to Tara, a serious look on her face.

"It won't be much longer now, Tara. I can feel it in my bones . . . the constant ache, the greater need for my pain medicine. I feel weaker every day. Soon I won't be able to rise from bed."

Tara stared at her, unsure of what to say. Claire continued.

"Your father had to carry me over to this chair today. He's been feeding me when the pain gets to be too much. I don't want anyone to see it. I don't want to be like Grandpa Jon," she said. Tara placed her hand gently on her mother's, which seemed to have aged twenty years in the past few weeks.

"You are *nothing* like Grandpa Jon. Grandpa Jon was an asshole," Tara said.

"Grandpa Jon *was* an asshole, wasn't he?" she replied with a giggle. Tara was so shocked that she could think of nothing to do but laugh along with her. Suddenly they were in a fit of uncontrollable laughter, clutching their sides and wiping tears from their eyes.

"Your father is such a better man than he ever was," Claire said as she wiped away the final remnants of laughter from her eyes. Tara said nothing, since she really didn't know who her father was.

"He's a lot like you, you know," Claire said softly. She gazed over at Tara.

"I know, I know. We look exactly the same," Tara said. She had been told this her whole life. Same nose, same eyes, same hair. Despite the times when he had been particularly distant in her youth, those days when she had wished that somehow her real parents were from a wizarding world and she would get to escape to them, she knew that there was no questioning where she came from.

"No, it's more than that," Claire said sternly. "You are both passionate about succeeding in life. You crave it. You're both kind and loving, and you stand up for your family. I don't — " She paused, her eyes squeezed shut as she fought off a wave of pain. After a moment, she opened her eyes. They were watery. Her resolve to continue the conversation won out, though she slumped a little deeper into her chair. "You're here, aren't you? I've watched you with your nieces, Tara. I see the longing in your eyes, the hope that you could give them what you didn't have. I'm not an idiot. I know the battle you're fighting."

"Is that why you brought me here? To try and force me to face my past?"

"No. I brought you here because I believe that there are still things here that you want, and because you're denying yourself happiness and giving power to the wrong people."

"I don't want anything here." It was Tara's natural instinct to deny any ties to her home or anything having to do with it. But Claire was unfazed.

"Don't you? Don't you want to watch Maddie grow into a beautiful young woman, a teenager who wants to talk to her aunt about boys when her mother wouldn't approve? Don't you want to live out your days with the handsome farmer?" she finished with a sly smirk. Tara rolled her eyes.

"Tom, the man you hand-selected and then sent out to woo me? That farmer?"

"Well, yes. But look at you both, Tara. Really. Take a good, hard look, and do it through my eyes — the eyes of a dying woman."

"Don't say that," Tara protested, pushing the thought away.

"If you were in my shoes, at the very end of your life, what would you wish you had done? What would fifty-year-old you make sure to tell you now?"

Tara sat in silence and considered her mother's words. "I honestly don't know," she said quietly. "I'm so confused."

Claire smiled and began to rock in her chair again. "Will you go get my purse, Tara? It's in my room, on the floor by the bed."

Though she was confused, she was in no position to question her mother's request. She ran back into the house and found the little brown purse exactly where she'd said it would be. She made her way back out to the porch and handed her the purse, but Claire shook her head.

"Open the large pouch, and look for a little purple bag," she said. Tara unzipped the silver zipper and spread the bag open to easily find a little purple drawstring pouch. She held it up.

"Now open it," she said.

Tara pulled apart the opening and tipped the bag over. Her grandmother's ring fell into her open hand. She stared at it with wide eyes. The large emerald glittered in the late-afternoon sunlight. As she tilted her hand, the small diamonds winked at her.

"You didn't really think I'd withhold it from you, did you?" Claire asked, staring intently at Tara as the meaning of the gesture registered. Slowly, she turned to look at her mother.

"I know how much she did for you, honey," Claire went on, seeing acceptance creep into her daughter's blue eyes. "I wanted to see you with it before things got bad."

Tara was jolted out of her reverie. "What do you mean 'bad'?" she asked, scared of the answer.

"You know what's coming, Tara. We all know cancer well enough to know that the end can come swiftly. Soon I'll lose my ability to speak, to rise, to eat. I've got my end-of-life session with your sister tonight after dinner, and then I'll be ready for whatever comes next."

Not really knowing how to respond to her mother's candid explanation of her terminal disease, Tara sat in silence for a minute and watched the afternoon pass in a slow haze. Finally, she asked quietly, "Does it hurt now?"

Claire offered a small smile that looked more like a grimace. "Terribly. It has for some time, though the meds have been helping to numb the pain. Your father's taken good care of me, Tara. I would like you to extend the same courtesy to him when I'm gone."

She tried not to imagine how she could possibly care for her father, the man she barely knew. She hoped that her future self would have a great solution for her mother's wishes, since her present self had none.

They spent the next two hours saying the things they had never wanted to say, forgiving the things they had never been willing to forgive. In these moments, Tara found it easy to speak with her. Claire had taken to her illness and subsequent demise with the ease of a mother preparing for childbirth. "Just another part of life," she'd said.

After all their words had been spoken, they sat in silence as the chirp of crickets began to permeate the air. The evening meal would be served soon, Tara's moments with her mother reaching their end. She sighed. In the distance, her sister's car was pulling up the drive.

"I'll miss you, Mom," Tara said. She reached over and lightly stroked her mother's hand.

Claire gave her fingers a light squeeze and said, "I'll miss you too, baby."

Dinner was noisy once again. Maddie demanded certain foods and forcefully pushed away others, while Emily cried until she was given a bottle and then slept peacefully. Tom entertained the group with wild stories of the reality-TV drama he'd witnessed among the goats — they'd kicked and bitten one another in the cattiest of ways. Tara watched her mother carefully out of the corner of her eye. Though she smiled softly at Tom's jokes, she did not laugh. Tara began to assume that she didn't because it would hurt too much, which broke her heart a little more.

The group went to the living room, where Tara, Michael, and Kaily took on Tom, Bob, Penny, and Ned for a rousing match of Pictionary. Naturally, being two of the most competitive people had led Michael and Tara to become the loudest protesters when they lost and the proudest winners at the end of the game. Tara fell back onto a sofa next to Tom, and they laughed wildly at the game-winning drawing: a stork, though it looked like some sort of modern art.

"How can you guess that in ten seconds?" Tom asked, gazing at Tara with admiration.

She lifted her chin proudly, glanced over at Michael, and said, "Michael and I just have that kind of connection, Tom. We are psychically linked."

"Damn right we are!" Michael proclaimed. He raised his glass and clinked it with Tara's triumphantly. As she took a healthy sip of her wine, her eyes wandered up to the kitchen door, where Ali was helping Claire to the bedroom. In the dim lighting, Tara could just make out Ali wiping a stray tear from her eye as she half-carried her. Tara looked over to her father, who had already noticed and was rising to join them.

"Thanks for dinner, Tom," he said politely.

"Good night, Dad," Tara said. He paused next to her on his way and gave her a side hug.

"Good night, squirt," he said.

Tara stared after him, and her mother's wish came back to mind. She was not at all sure how they would go on without her mother as a buffer. Whenever she wanted to talk to her father, she talked to her mother. Then, Claire would transmit the message, gather a response, and send the missive over. It was the way it had always been . . . but now it would have to change. Tara was afraid of what would happen to that delicate system. Could she even talk to him? They barely understood each other as it was.

Her sister came out of the room shortly after her father disappeared and prepared the girls to go home. Tara helped her load them into the car, since Harold was at a book-club meeting and hadn't come join in the festivities.

"What did she tell you?" Tara asked quietly. Ali took her time strapping Emily in as Tara gave Maddie her pacifier, an object that was usually forbidden unless there was an emergency. She considered this an emergency.

"She told me goodbye," Ali said softly. Her face crumpled in grief, and she threw her hand up to her eyes to hide her devastation. Tara closed the car door quietly and then made her way over to the other side. Ali hugged Tara tightly and wept quietly for a minute before taking a deep breath and sliding into the driver's seat. It was The Kingston Way: Emotions are not allowed more than five minutes of prime time, and then it never happened.

"Will you keep me posted?" Ali asked. She reached into her purse for a tissue and gave her nose a quick blow. Tara promised that she would.

"Are you okay to drive?" she asked. Ali waved a hand dismissively.

"Of course I am. I'll text you when I get home."

"All right." Tara watched the car drive away and dissolve into the darkness. She reached into her pocket and felt the cold stones of her grandmother's ring. She didn't know what to do with it. Tara let the stones dig deep into her hand, imagining the cut that would bleed if her family's emerald were to etch itself into her palm. She wondered whether her hand had any right to grace that gem. Tara Kingston, the family outsider. What right did she have to carry the weight of a family she had avoided?

She shivered even though the late July air was warm and dry. Gazing up at the sky, she watched the stars blink at her, as they had blinked at billions upon billions of people throughout time. Had she seen these exact stars in another life? Would her mother be reborn and gaze at them in a different form with the same sense of utter inadequacy that Tara felt now?

She felt, rather than heard, Tom come up behind her. She knew it was him, because, these days, she always knew when it was him. He had hovered at her door nightly, waiting for a chance to be a part of her life, her world. Would she open up a space for him and let him in? She still didn't know. Although he was wonderful to her, well-loved by her family, and a man who knew how to cook (how rare and wonderful!), he was still *here*. Wrong place, wrong time.

Tara thought about Boston and how few of these stars she was able to see there. Would it be the same after this? In such a short

amount of time, her entire world had shifted, and she felt without a
home and without a path to get to one. Her mind buzzed with a
hollow emptiness as she stoodin the dirt in front of the purple
farmhouse, waiting for her mother to die just a few rooms away.

"Mind if we take a seat?" Tom hesitated to ask. Tara shook her
head, waving her hand for him to join her as she plopped down in the
dirt. They sat side by side in the pitch-black dark of night, staring up at
the half orb of sky beyond the Rocky Mountains around them.

Finally, Tara broke the silence. "You're really close to my mom,
huh?"

"No more than anyone else, really," he replied nonchalantly.

"Yes, you are," she insisted. She wished she had brought her
wine glass out with her. She liked having something to sip on during
these types of conversations, something to break her tension. Tom
shrugged but said nothing.

"Will you tell me something — truthfully?" she asked, gazing at
his silhouette.

"Of course," he replied, placing his palms behind him in the dirt
and leaning back to get a better view of the night sky.

"Was she . . . happy? Those years I was away?"

Tom sighed, which made her feel edgy. That was obviously a no.

"She was . . .," he said slowly, as though trying to find the best
way to describe Claire. "She smiled and laughed a lot, but I know that
she missed you. She felt responsible for you leaving."

Tara couldn't help the simultaneous pangs of guilt and envy she
felt at hearing these words — guilt for leaving, envy for her mother
having confided in Tom and not been honest with her. Claire had
never found it so easy to confide in Tara like that, or so it had
seemed.

"She wasn't," Tara replied. "I wish her letters would have said
that. I wish she could have just said she was sorry, rather than heaping
all the blame on me." She let her emotions pour out freely, no longer
able to hold everything back.

"I think she wishes that, too," he replied, shifting his hand over to cover hers. For some reason, this small gesture of intimacy made Tara's eyes well up, and she fought her tears back.

"Do you know what you're going to do . . . after?" Tom asked, a small amount of fear registering in his usually confident voice. It was then Tara realized that Tom wanted her to stay much more than he had let on. She could feel the ring in her pocket pressing against her thigh, a sign of commitment she had never known how to give. She was under no obligation to stay here. Her mother's manipulation was meant to keep her around long enough to fall in love with Tom and stay. She held no delusion about that and had been actively trying not to resent Tom for it. He had played her into his hands, and even if he'd done it for the right reasons, he'd still done it. Where was the trust in that?

"I don't know," she replied. It was the honest truth. His hand stiffened ever so slightly on hers. She wanted to pull away, to tell him that he had no right to do what they had all done: make her feel guilty for living her own life.

"You know, you could stay, Tara. You belong here . . ."

"I *don't* belong here. I know it gets a little cloudy and hard to remember, but if you recall the first time we met, when you were manipulating me to want to stay, I told you that." She couldn't quite keep the venom out of her voice, and suddenly, she didn't want to.

"I wasn't manipulating you. I . . .," Tom protested, but Tara interjected.

"I have spent my entire life being told that I am wrong. I grew up wrong. I dressed wrong. I went to school in the wrong place. I'm wrong for being happy somewhere else. You come along with the intention of proving their point, and somehow that makes you the savior of the day? Now we can live happily ever after on your quaint little farm, just like you planned?" Tears were running a neat little path down to her chin. She wiped them away, her palm swiping against her face.

"I don't think you're wrong, Tara. I think you're delusional." She was surprised by the rush of anger in his voice. It fueled her own, and she was ready to step up to bat.

"Excuse me?" she said, goading him on. Deluded, was she? She was ready to hear just what he had to say about that. She had been preparing for this fight, this accusation, for years; she had just expected it to be with her aunts rather than the man she had fancied herself half in love with. He turned and looked down at her, his eyes fierce even in the dark.

"You have convinced yourself that Colorado is the worst place to live in the entire world based solely on the acts of two self-absorbed, insecure aunts. You didn't fit in as a child. Big whoop, Tara. *No one* fits in as a child. That's called life. You have seen the power of human healing all summer long; you have spent time with your sister and watched your nieces grow with open happiness — I've watched every minute of it. And when it comes down to the wire, you'd rather live your whole life away from them because you are too blind to see that doing that makes your aunts the winners and you a sore loser."

Tara looked up at him in stunned silence.

"Why can't you *see* that, Tara? Why can't you let yourself heal and take control of your own life?" Tom continued, his voice edgy as he fought to get through to her. "They have been controlling you all this time. Tell me that you hate this farm, that my mother and our friends here have made your life miserable, and you can't wait to get on a plane and never see us again. You tell me that now and I will let you go and wish you the best, but I don't believe it — not for a second. I love you, Tara. I've loved you since I heard your sad little tale at the bar in Chicago, and I wanted so badly to hold you and put you in a world where you could find happiness and feel whole. Why won't you let yourself? Why?"

Tara felt as though she'd been slapped. Why couldn't she let herself be happy? Why did she insist on living alone if it meant that she wouldn't have to face a small group of people she could have been brave enough to let go of in the first place?

"I don't know how," she whispered. Tom heaved a sigh, his frustration burning out as fast as it had arrived. How did he manage to do that?

"Will you let us try and help you figure that out, Tara?"

Her eyes strained to read his in the darkness. The two of them had a lot to survive before she would ever be whole again. The worst part was that her mother wouldn't be here to see it.

"Let's take care of my mother first, please," she begged. "Then we can work on whatever's going on with me."

"Fair enough." He hefted himself up and reached out a hand. She placed her hand in his and gripped it hard. He was sturdy and stable, a lifeline that she had never opted to use before. She pulled herself up and brushed the dirt from her jeans, and they made their way back to the house, not noticing Penny's silhouette watching them from an open side window. She let out a breath, glanced up at the sky and then dropped the drapes and turned away.

That night, Tom did not linger by Tara's door. She lay awake and alone, churning his words over and over in her mind. She thought of her mother and father, the way she had been treated growing up. There was no excuse for it, but Tom was right. She had let it define her all her adult life, and it was time to make her own decisions, even if it meant rethinking everything she had led herself to believe.

•••

Chapter Sixteen

Tara was a little girl again, in her Gran's house.

"What's this, Gran?"

She was digging in some old boxes in the attic, delighting in the stale smell of the old and forgotten. There was something about it that made her feel alive, like she could be part of the past. It was her favorite game of pretend. She held up a small picture frame with an important-looking document inside. Gran walked over and sat on the floor next to her.

"That is my degree," she said. "Did you know that when I was a young woman, going to college was something only men were supposed to do?"

Tara wrinkled her nose. "Why? I'm really good at school, and I'm a girl."

Alice smiled. "I know you are, baby girl, and I'm glad. Well, you wouldn't believe it, but I applied to college anyway and got in. Of course, it was an all-girls school, but I made some of my best friends those few years."

Tara stared at the degree, searching for a word that would be easy to read despite the difficult cursive font so she could impress her grandmother. "Bos . . . ton," she sounded out slowly. "Boston?" She looked up into her grandmother's eyes for validation.

"That's right! Boston." Tara beamed and said the word a few more times. "Boston, Boston, Boston! I want to go there!"

"It's a wonderful place where this country's Founding Fathers spent a lot of time. You remember the story of George Washington and Thomas Jefferson?"

Tara nodded. Suddenly, she rose up. "I'm going to go to school in Boston, too, just like you, Gran!"

Gran laughed. "Well, you have a bit of time to decide on that one, Tar bear."

Tara shook her head stubbornly. "I'm going to Boston, and you'll come with me and Mom and Ali and Dad," she spouted, excited over her plans to leave with everyone in her life who mattered to her. Gran frowned.

"Now, why would you say a thing like that?" Tara looked down and shuffled her feet, like she would get in trouble for her answer.

"Tara Kingston, you tell me why you want to leave right now," Gran demanded. Tara sighed, serious as a six-year-old can be.

"None of the kids at school are really nice to me. Maybe people in Boston will be my friend."

Gran frowned and reached for a piece of Tara's silky brown hair, stroking it lovingly. "You'll find your place in this world, Tara, and when you do, you won't want it any other way."

"I don't think so, Gran. I want to go away with you and Mom and Dad and Ali."

Gran sighed. This was one argument she wouldn't be winning.

"Well, you might at that," she said. "But remember, Tara, someday you might just find something here worth staying for."

Tara shook her head. "I don't think so."

Gran hid a smile. *Ah, to have the wisdom of a six-year-old*, she thought.

"If you say so, darling. If you say so."

Claire's health deteriorated precisely as she had predicted. They spent days by her bedside, either watching her sleep or chatting quietly when she felt up to talking. Tara had never seen her father in such a state — dark bags had formed under his eyes, and he had lost a considerable amount of weight himself. He barely touched the delicious food that Penny and Tom whipped up. Tara had no idea what to say or do.

Penny and Tom were the glue holding everyone together. They put most of the farm duties on Michael and Kaily's shoulders to help them get the practice, and they in turn kept Ned in line. He had matured rapidly over the summer, and his nights of drinking and partying were reserved only for when the following day could be spent in recovery. Michael and Kaily worked well together, and they were quiet and stoic when surrounded by the grieving family.

Claire had made an explicit request that only immediate family be allowed to visit her at the farm until she died.

"I won't have drama in my final moments," she said simply. "Only love."

This was what she had on the final day in late August when her last rattling breath came and went. Tara sat by her bedside, holding her frail hand and wishing that they could have said just a few more words to each other. She glanced over at her father, who held his wife's other hand and stared at her in utter disbelief. Tara had watched her father dote on her mother all her life, treating her with an affection and attention he gave to no one else. The rest of his family was given duty and respect, but not the kind of love he showered on Claire. Tara began to cry as she watched his face crumple inward. In the silence of Claire's room, Bob's sobs echoed around them. He fell to his knees and buried his forehead on the bed next to Claire's body.

No one touched him. It was as though time had turned to molasses. Every passing second became a distinct frame that would be burned into their memories forever.

They had already arranged for her cremation, since she would not allow the arrangements to be a burden. Tara's father had made the appropriate calls. He left with her mother's body, and it became Tara and her farm friends once again.

The house was quiet. Dinners were quiet with murmurs and procedure rather than the usual buoyant joy. From the day her mother had taken a turn for the worse until the end, Tom had been Tara's rock, letting her cry and grieve in any way she needed. In the week preceding the funeral, he helped her keep busy — did anything to prevent her from constantly thinking about it. Finally, Tara found herself draping another black funeral dress over her shoulders and preparing to drive back to Littleton for the ceremony. Tom knocked on her door quietly to see if she was ready to go.

"Yes, just one more thing," she said as she walked over to the side table and opened the wooden drawer to reveal her grandmother's ring. She slid it onto her right hand and pulled her hand tight into a fist. She needed her grandmother here with her today, and knowing that her mother had been the ring's keeper for so long gave her the feeling of having her closer.

Tom and Tara drove down to the house in Littleton, and Tara was amazed at how it seemed like it'd been so long since she had been exposed to other people. Being surrounded by major grocery stores, banks, and never-ending paved roads made her feel suffocated, and she longed to turn back and go to the farm again . . . to live out those peaceful summer days with her mother.

When they got to the house, the whole family was there, appropriately dressed in black. Her aunts had chosen low-cut designer dresses for the event, and Tara's body tensed at the sight of them. Tom squeezed her hand — a reminder. She glanced at him with a small excuse for a smile and tried repeating to herself the loaded words he had tossed at her that night on the bench. It was now her task and her task alone to not let them impact her, and she hoped fervently that she was strong enough to do so.

Tara searched the large, open first floor for her father or sister and found him sitting on the edge of a couch alone, watching something on TV. They made their way over and sat next to him.

"Everything ready?" Tara asked.

"Yeah," he said, glancing over for a split second with glazed eyes. "Your sister offered to speak for the small ceremony, and then we'll take her into the mountains to be . . . spread." Tara reached over and patted his hand. He looked over at her, desperation in his eyes.

"What am I going to do without her, Tara?" he asked, choking on the words.

It scared her. She had never seen her father as anything but capable. The concept of having to support him was foreign. Still, this was an opportunity for her to step into her new self. She looked him squarely in the eyes with as much confidence as she could muster and replied, "We'll figure it out."

Ali spoke eloquently of their mother. Sniffles filled the room, and tissues were handed around generously. Bob was stoic. He took it all in and said nothing for fear of choking up in front of everyone. Those who wanted to share a memory of Claire said their piece, and then the gathering broke, and small clusters of people came together, waiting for the group to leave with her ashes. Tara tensed when she was approached by Marilyn and Jo.

"Your mother was a wonderful woman, Tara. You were lucky to have her," Marilyn said as she dabbed a tissue at her perfectly dry eyes. Tara's expression stayed solemn and unreadable.

"I was," she replied. They were annoyed that she wasn't taking the bait.

"It's unfortunate that you lost so much time with her, being gone and all. I hope this has taught you where your priorities lie," Jo goaded. Tara smiled sadly and patted her lightly on the shoulder.

"We got it back this summer. It helped that she insisted on having her actual family with her in the end. She also gave me her full blessing to cut you both out of my life forever, so I actually have something to look forward to now."

"You are one sad little girl," Marilyn said. Tara stared at her for a minute, watching her shift her weight from one black stiletto to another. They really did get satisfaction simply from these types of comments. For the first time ever, she began to feel pity for them.

"No," she said, taking Tom's hand in hers. "It's not me who's the sad one. Marilyn, I hope your husband finds the strength to stop preying on teenage girls. And Jo, I hope you learn to be your own person instead of being Marilyn's lackey. It doesn't suit you at all. Best of luck to you both." She gave them a brief nod before turning away, but not before memorizing the shock painted on their faces and taking a little satisfaction that she would forever have the last word.

"Feel better?" Tom whispered into her ear.

"I'll feel better when we get out of here and can go back home." He paused. "Home?"

She gave his hand a small squeeze. "I've got a proposition for you, but let's talk about it later. We need to take Mom to her final resting place."

Bob Kingston stood on a small bridge in Boulder delicately holding his wife's remains like a precious gift. He didn't know how to let her go despite having tried to prepare himself for this event for years. It was just as terrible as he'd believed it would be, and the thought of driving back to their home alone made his stomach queasy. He felt supported with his children standing on either side of him. Claire would live on through them — they spoke and laughed just like her. He tried to take comfort in that.

Ali stepped a little closer and stared into the rushing waters.

"Ready?" she asked quietly.

"Yes." He wasn't and never would be. Still, far be it from him to ever say no to Claire Kingston. He carefully uncorked her cobalt-colored urn and gave up some room for Ali and Tara to help him release their mother's spirit into the water. The three of them tipped the ashes in and watched as Claire floated away. She was gone in an instant. They stared after the rushing current, as if by doing so, Claire would somehow walk back up the stream and tease them for looking so foolish.

She did not. Minutes passed, and finally Ali patted her father's shoulder and walked away. Tara stayed and stood close to him.

"You got plans after this, Dad?" she asked. He shook his head. He had no plans for anything anymore.

"I'd like to ask you something, and it's okay if you say no," she said, still staring into the water. He brought himself back to the present to hear what she had to say.

"What's that, squirt?"

"I'd like you to come and live with us at the farm."

He looked at her then, her eyes a reflection of his own, so alike and yet so vastly different they had been.

"I figured you'd be leaving soon," he said. He'd expected it of her, after all.

Tara shrugged. "Well, I've done some thinking, and of all the most ridiculous things . . . Mom was right. Tom has offered me a home, and I intend to take him up on it."

Bob whistled. "She sure has a way of getting things done, doesn't she?" He was unwilling to talk about Claire in the past tense yet.

Tara laughed. "She always did. Come stay with us. Please," she said, frail hope cresting her eyes.

He gazed back into the waters. Of course, he knew his answer; Claire had left no stone unturned. He liked the farm and enjoyed the peacefulness of the scenery. It was the last place they had lived together as a family.

"I think I can do that," he said.

Tara's eyes shimmered with unshed tears, and she wrapped her arms around her father. He hugged her back just as tightly. After a moment she pulled away, swiping at her eyes.

"On one condition . . .," Tara said.

He leaned toward her and raised an eyebrow.

"No Marilyn or Jo there, Dad. If you want to see them, you'll have to go down there. I don't want them in my life."

Bob heaved a sigh, exhausted with the weight of the world. If his sisters refused to treat his child with the respect he demanded of them, then he saw no other choice. She deserved to be happy, and if keeping them away meant that she would be a part of his life, this was the only way to keep both of his worlds somewhat together.

He nodded. "Done."

Tom walked up to them and snuck an arm around Tara's shoulders. She nestled into him.

"Looks like we're starting a new chapter for the Kingston family, Tom Sanders," she said.

Tom's face lit up, and he clenched his fists in excitement. He looked at Bob and leveled his gaze as he said, "When my dad died, my mom and I were pretty lost. But then we learned how to heal and regrow together. I'd be honored if you could trust us with that process. We'd love to help." He held out a hand for Bob to shake.

"That sounds great," Bob said, clasping his hand in Tom's. In spite of his grief, his grip was strong as ever.

They began to make their way back to Bob's shiny new car and Tom's small red truck.

"I've got to go get some things in order," Bob said as he opened the car door.

"All right," Tara said. "We'll see you at home."

•••

Acknowledgments

First and foremost, I must give my profound thanks to my brilliant and amazing editor, Alissa Stevens. This book would not be what it is without her keen insight and general awesomeness. I'd also like to thank everyone at Creators Publishing for taking a chance on this book.

Thank you to my parents, Mike and Diane. I wouldn't be who I am today without your guidance and wisdom. Thank you to my husband, Shane, my rock, my universe, my infinity love. I survive the challenges life throws at me only because I have you by my side.

Last but not least, thank you, dear reader, for purchasing this book. I hope that you liked it, and that it maybe spoke to you in some way. Keep tough and stay positive — the universe works in amazing ways.

About the Author

Shana Chartier is a New England author, librarian, wife, mother, and cat mom. She has written in several genres, including poetry; children's picture books; short fiction in romance, fantasy, and contemporary genres; young adult fiction; new adult fiction; and now women's fiction. Her debut novel, *Past Lives,* was nominated for a New Hampshire Literary Award for outstanding young adult literature.

Shana's world revolves around writing. She is a former ghostwriter who wrote over twenty books in 2017 alone, several of which have landed on Amazon's best-seller list. By day, she's a librarian at Southern New Hampshire University and a writing coach for aspiring authors. When she has free time, she tends to spend it watching terrible television or going on adventures with family.

HOME
is also available as an e-book
for Kindle, Amazon Fire, iPad, Nook and
Android e-readers. Visit
creatorspublishing.com to learn more.

o o o

CREATORS PUBLISHING

We find compelling storytellers and
help them craft their narrative,
distributing their novels and collections
worldwide.

o o o